I0597956

# A Heart Never Heals

A Novel by

# George Delmarmo

**CCB Publishing**
**British Columbia, Canada**

A Heart Never Heals

Copyright ©2005, 2010, 2014 by George Delmarmo
ISBN-13   978-1-77143-166-8
Third Edition

Library and Archives Canada Cataloguing in Publication
Delmarmo, George, 1936-, author
A heart never heals / written by George Delmarmo. -- Third edition.
Issued in print and electronic formats.
ISBN 978-1-77143-166-8 (pbk.).--ISBN 978-1-77143-167-5 (pdf)
Additional cataloguing data available from Library and Archives Canada

Contact the author George Delmarmo at: Hogfarmer@aol.com

Publisher:   CCB Publishing
             British Columbia, Canada
             www.ccbpublishing.com

# Contents

# Characters

George
Betsy
Cardinal Carmine
Mr. Fields
Russ
Harry
Mrs. Smith
Tony
Henry
Mr. Wilson
Angelo Raimo
Marino family
Sabatini
Maria

# Prologue

Depending on one's field of study the correlation between logic and common sense becomes more closely aligned. One has an experience that defies logic and makes absolutely no sense when compared to generally accepted principles that we refer to as common sense.

Each of us deals with our emotions based upon our religious and family upbringing. Each person has his own expectations of what love is or will be and at the same time tries to avoid the dreaded loneliness that lurks behind every corner. What a person expects from either of these emotions is further heightened by what is taught in schools in the formal sense and what one perceives it should be from the results of listening to the "teachers" of "peer pressure." Does one hide from the rages of love? Those hidden fears that will make you do anything to achieve it or feel it. To become so obsessed with the thoughts of being with someone that it engulfs your very being. The problem becomes more complex as the definition of love becomes further defined with the fears that it brings. The greatest fear becomes, "What is life like if love never happens?" At some point one realizes that loneliness has the same symptoms. The feelings are the same. The search will put you on the opposite end of a mythical yardstick while at the same time binding your emotions together since the results are exactly the same…the burning physical and mental need to be with a certain person, one that it may take years to find while being constantly plagued by the fear that they will never be found or even if the person exists at all.

Such is the situation with one of the characters, George. George was born and raised in a little town of Belleville, a suburb of a larger town. Words such as bias, prejudice and harassment had not found their way into anyone's vocabulary. Being of Italian decent had little effect upon his values in any major way since he was raised American in America.

The public school system was considered by most people to be superior to the ones in surrounding towns. The town itself was started on the Passaic River and expanded up from there in a hit or miss fashion. The town was one large farm after another but these soon gave way to immigrants from many countries but mostly from Italy. The yearly feasts, honoring the various saints, drew large crowds of Italians and Italian American visitors. There was an abundance of churches in the area. The moral standard of the Catholic Church was by far the most predominate. The schools taught the customary ABCs and while the teachers tried to instill in the students a desire to learn, the Catholic Church taught "the difference between Heaven and Hell" as postulated by the Ten Commandments. Children started school in the first grade, unlike today where there is pre-school and kindergarten before one finally enters the first grade. Women raised their children rather than pawn them off to a child-raising factory. Love was a four-letter word, which was not used too often since the connotation of it made young girls blush openly while young men blushed privately. No one ever knows what the word love means to anyone else but the teaching and acceptance of a situation concludes, "They're in love." Since one never experiences anything like love before he or she becomes befuddled and in awe of the feeling, each person feels that to be truly in love is to exclude all others for the benefit of one. The church is very insistent upon this.

This book, when finished, will represent the sum total of the experiences one can have while examining his sanity and feelings. When I first experienced a sense of someone else's emotions, I dismissed it as a young man's foolishness. As the years started to go by, each additional incident was similarly dismissed. As one gets older and faces the challenges and opportunities that are placed before him or else is confronted by him it becomes easier to put on a mantel of indifference or callousness and just concentrate on a career or family. Anything that interferes with either of the objectives is dismissed as being plain silly.

I guess, as everyone else who has gone through the rigors of the education process, we have all wondered whether or not there is such a thing as extra sensory perception. In Psychology I or II everyone reads about mental telepathy experiments but the results of such tests are soon dismissed as being ridiculous.

The basic religious training teaches its students about visions and sightings. The reality of something like these events taking place seems remote at best. The problem with believing such things is usually compounded by everyone around you not believing, or else, being very logical and applying their good "common sense" which they feel can explain everything away. There is always a "logical explanation" if one just takes their time searching for it. It is against this type of background that this book was written. It started out as a letter to no one and just kept growing. I preface this book by saying I have tried as much as possible to stick to "the facts and only the facts."

Another person's feelings were somehow transmitted by some power or conduit to me. That, at first, fascinated me and finally, haunted me. The experience became so intense that it dominated my being. I guess as any other well educated, mature individual, it took a long time to accept what was happening. I put my skepticism aside and recorded what was happening to me. Most of the time the words I was writing made me feel embarrassed and uneasy.

For this book to have any true meaning one must first recognize that life is not always a straightforward thing. The events that took place happened while I was working on a case that had nothing to do with her. Both events were occurring simultaneously. There was, as far as I could see, no reason why one event or experience should have any effect on the other. The only common denominator I could ever find was the element of time. They happened during the same time in my life. The case ended, but the feelings and thoughts continue.

We first met in the seventh grade. We were in some of each other's classes through high school. She was not the "pin up" type, nor did she have those qualities that would have distinguished her in a crowd. Her personality was warm, but did not discern her in any form. After high school she attended a small college in Pennsylvania and became a teacher. Because of her easy and warm ways she was drawn to teaching children with special needs.

It seems that while she attended college her life was peaceful. She was married and had two children. The marriage ended in divorce. Of course, I didn't know that at that time, but now as I have researched her life I am able to explain why at certain times in my life I had experiences that I couldn't explain at the time they happened and have a hard time understanding or explaining them now.

I hope that this book will help other people who find themselves in a similar situation to have a better insight and be able to deal with it more expeditiously than I could. Whatever literary freedom I've taken was done to make the story more readable. But the truth was never totally abandoned.

The unexplained event happened while I was in Italy working on an assignment. I felt very tired and decided to rest a couple of days before returning home. I was staying at a hotel in Salerno and asked the clerk if there were any non-tourist resorts where I could go. He immediately named one and quickly wrote down the directions for me getting there. He called the owner who was a friend of his and the next morning I was on my way. The drive took a couple of hours. After I checked in and spent the day walking around the little town I returned to the hotel. There were very few guests staying in the hotel so I invited the owner and his dining room people to dinner. The owner was surprised at the invitation but accepted. His contribution to the meal would be his own homemade wine and liquor. The chef promised a meal that would be better than any I ever had. That evening, after my walk and afternoon nap, we assembled in a private dining room and the feast and the story, "The Heart Never Heals" begins.

# Chapter One

"George, George you don't like the wine?" The speaker was the owner of a resort located about 50 miles south of Salerno, Italy. How and why I was there on this muggy evening in September will be explained later in the story. It was the off-season for the resort so that I was given the honor of having dinner with the owner, head chef and the maître d'. The owner was very proud of his new wine and the liquor he had distilled from it. He explained the process to me but his English was limited and my Italian non-existent so I just sampled everything many times. It seemed, as my glass got empty it would refill itself. The meal consisted of everything the chef knew how to make. He would introduce each new dish with a detailed explanation as to its contents and the care and method of preparation. The dinner was lasting well into the night. Finally, I had had enough.

"My friend, the wine is great. The meal something else, but I have had enough. I will now bid you nice people good night." As I spoke, I got up from the table in one movement that surprised me. The fact that I could move at all was a shock.

As I left my dinner guests all said "goodnight." Their voices came through a foggy haze. I made my way back to my room. I tried to get undressed, but the wine and liquor was taking a toll. I lay on the bed for a few minutes. About three hours later I woke up as though I were being called. I sat up in bed. I had to wait a few minutes for my head to clear. I felt extremely uncomfortable as the room seemed to close in on me. The window in my room was open and I could feel the soft warm breeze that was blowing. I decided I would take a walk on the beach. I washed my face to clear my head. The coolness of the water made me feel somewhat alive. I changed into a pair of shorts, t-shirt and sandals. The hotel was very quiet as I made my way outside on to the gray, sandy beach at this Mediterranean resort. It was a dark night, for the moon seemed to have abandoned the earth. I could hear the waves of the Mediterranean Sea playing a hypnotic tune on the beach. With the sound as my guide I made my way down to the water.

As I looked back towards the hotel it loomed out of the night like a great monster. It was a one-story building that seemed to go on forever. As I faced the grand hotel from the beach, the memory of my arrival came back to me. As I looked at the building, to my left was the entrance way and the large circular driveway that I had entered through when I had arrived. The first section of the building was the entrance lobby which was decorated with an elaborate display of Italian art. It included many paintings and sculptures of local artists. Each of the local artists had had a hand in decorating the lobby that looked more like a large gift shop than a lobby to a resort hotel. There were price tags on everything. Any interest that was shown towards any item was immediately encouraged by a staff member with a detailed explanation of the item of interest and a brief description of the artist. As an additional inducement an explanation of the owner's deep concern for the arts and the local artist was added. It was as though the staff was apologizing for the appearance of the lobby even though I was truly in awe of it. I didn't buy anything, but I liked it. After I had registered I was led through a long hallway towards my room that was at the far end of the hotel. I had to walk past a large banquet hall, bar and dining room. As I was led past each room my guide pointed out everything to me. Every door opened out onto a patio with a clear view of the Mediterranean Sea. I was told that each guest room also had a clear view of the water. When I was finally at my room, the sliding doors opened out on to a patio which ran the entire length of the complex. Now that I had viewed it from my vantage point by the sea at night, the hotel looked much bigger. The evening lights on the building gave me confidence that I would be able to find it again, especially since there was nothing else around.

I walked further down right to the edge of the water and I looked out into the blackness that shrouded the Mediterranean. I could hear the waves beating a rhythmic tune on the shore as I felt the water hitting my toes through my open sandals. The sound was my guide, for nothing else could be seen. The combination of the melodious tune and the absence of light had a sort of hypnotical effect on me as each part of my consciousness began to shut down. The gentle breeze that was blowing accented the solitude I felt as it swirled about me searching for a place to settle. I saw something coming out of the water towards the beach. I could not recognize what it was. The thing started to take on the shape of a human the closer it got. Suddenly, it was in front of me. I had to blink to bring my eyes into focus for I feared what I saw. For a split moment I lost consciousness. I was again alert.

She was there.

Betsy.

The person whose presence I felt on my boat back in the states.

The person I felt near me back at the racetrack.

Betsy.

The world stood still.

The air left.

Breathing was impossible.

Time was non-existent

Betsy filled the great void that was left.

In a split second everything I thought I had accomplished in my life up to that point had a zero value. My academic degrees meant nothing, for I realized that they were obtained not by a desire to acquire knowledge but to fill the void in my life that for the first time I realized was caused by the absence of Betsy.

At that moment in time I felt all the fears and hurt that loneliness can unleash upon a person. Whatever I was and whatever I could be was washed away by the relentless beating of the waves upon the shore. The gentle breeze had now turned more violent and acted as an additional cleanser, as it too helped deprive me of all the thoughts that I held dear. Everything in my world had been reduced to zero. I knew at that moment I was a mere man who wanted nothing else in life except to be loved by one person, Betsy. Her image had been made all the brighter by the blackness that surrounded her. In this instant she took the place of the gentle sounds of the waves and the gentle feeling of the wind. She had replaced all the natural elements.

I stood there shaking and had to call upon all my physical and mental strength and wisdom to make me realize that what I thought I saw was only a mirage. The trouble was that I didn't believe it. I said out loud, "She was there." The breeze was still blowing. The blackness was still black. The water was still gently lapping the shore. I quickly concluded that what I saw was the effects of the new wine the hotel manager had poured so generously. Added to that was the new liquor he had distilled from the September harvest. I shrugged my shoulders as a chilling breeze made my skin tense. The September night air all of a sudden had gotten cold. I started to feel silly as I tried to remember what caused my mouth to go dry and make my fist clench so tightly that I drove my nail right into my skin. "I'm nuts!" I shouted as I turned to return to my room. I felt I was retreating from some great battle I had yet to fight. My pace quickened as I sought the safety of my room. I felt some strange thing following me. I thought, "I'll be safe in my room."

As I entered the hotel, the night manager was there to greet me with another sampling of the wine and liquor, but I refused, for I had to get to my room. Once inside my room, I felt very cold as I undressed to get into the warmth of the bed. I suddenly realized that I had left my sandals on the beach, but the only thing I could think of doing at that moment was to reach the warmth and safety of the bed linens. I wrapped the bed linens tightly around me as though they were some sort of armor that would protect me from whatever this thing was that I felt. I fell into a sort of trance that left me fully conscious but unable to move.

She was there in my bedroom, Betsy. Betsy...that was her name...Betsy. The thought of her name started tolling in my head like a bell in a tower that kept getting closer. Betsy.

My room was enormous with a king-sized bed and one wall completely covered with mirrors and pictures. I really didn't know what time it was but it must have been late, I guess. I was afraid to go to sleep and more frightened to stay awake. I finally lay back and closed my eyes. I must have dozed off, but woke with a start...Betsy was there, just as she looked or as I remember she looked in school. I didn't know why, but she was crying. The vision frightened me so much that I just couldn't sit still. I didn't know what to do. I thought I had lost my mind. The whole experience had completely unnerved me. I sat there like a robot. I got up and walked around the room as though I was searching for something. I lay back down; afraid to close my eyes, for fear that she would re-appear while at the same time more afraid she wouldn't. The air in the room was gone.

Time and space became one. In this suspension I saw a young girl printing in old English letters, "In the Spring a young man's fancy lightly turns to thoughts of love." When she was done she faced the class and recited the opening passage from "Jane Eyre."

As I watched I was trembling. Thankfully, I fell onto the bed and lapsed into a deep sleep. The sleep which I thought would protect me quickly abandoned me as I lay in bed in some sort of stupor that I didn't understand. Many times I had been in dangerous situations and even some that were mind-boggling but I was not able to deal with the two new words that had entered my life for the first time, Love and Fear. Both of these intruders were not the kind I could face head on and do them battle. They were inside me. They were occupying a space that was all too foreign to me. I asked myself how I could overcome a fear of being in love when I did not know what that was. At an early age one is expected to be inexperienced in such matters. At 55 I was expected to be the teacher not the student. Having to deal with an emotion that I never had experienced before was what was causing the anxiety that was in me. Dealing with a new feeling and a new fear in this foreign land was just too much for me. I had to leave. I had to get home and be in my familiar surroundings. I could deal with this affliction as soon as I was in my territory. I kept trying to convince myself that I could overcome this new feeling once I was home while at the same time being in fear that I would win. A victory was starting to frighten me more for I felt that loneliness would again revisit me. I had been alone many times and in fact most of the time preferred it. This was the first time I was alone and felt lonely and I did not like the new experience. Finally my ally, sleep, came back to rescue me.

The next morning I tried to understand what had happened to me. I became frightened all over again, for I wasn't sure I wanted to know the answer. I was ashamed to admit I liked the feeling of having the sight of someone raise me to a height that I had never been to before. One person, whose mere presence made my entire body tingle, made me wonder if that was the feeling one feels when one is in love. Love, the sound of this new word frightened me less each time I said it. But was what I was feeling, love, or just the after effects of wine and liquor? The fact I was, for the first time questioning myself was creating the fear that I felt. I dismissed the whole matter from my mind as so much nonsense. The problem now became, I did not want this new feeling to go. I thought with time I would be able to rationalize the events that occurred. I sat down in the most comfortable chair, leaned back and let my thoughts drift into a private place within my mind.

A knocking on the door interrupted my solitude. When I asked who it was, I found out it was the manager delivering my breakfast. He became my distraction. I had forgotten that the night before I bet the manager that I could solve some riddle he had and the stake was breakfast in bed. He was a man of his word as he made my breakfast and now was delivering it. I unlocked the door and he let himself in. He wheeled the breakfast cart to the table in the room and set it for two as I quickly put on some clothes. The breakfast consisted of coffee, buns, cheeses, figs and jams. He was a pleasant man but that morning I couldn't wait for him to leave. Finally, the coffee was done and I convinced him I didn't want any of his liquor so he finally left. Alone at last I walked out on to the balcony of my room and looked out into the Mediterranean as the sunlight lit it up and the gentle blowing breeze all tried to make up for the previous night. As I drained the last drop of the bitter coffee from the cup I tried again to understand what happened to me on the beach. I realized that logic for the first time must be pushed aside. I was being forced into a realm where the real world had become unreal. There were no visible enemies to fight. Nothing external happened. I was transformed into a world where physical strength is unimportant and a keen mind only intensifies the experience. For the first time I tried to use prayer as a weapon but it was to no avail.

All the solutions to my problems that I had learned over the years seemed to have evaporated. I found myself floating in someplace that was neither heaven nor hell. Being torn between two places that are on the separate ends of some imaginary place that when stretched creates a vacuum. I now realize that I was somewhere in that vacuum.

There was nothing real to hang on to and worse yet, I didn't want to be saved. I was in some new place and instead of resisting I was more than anxious to go. It was like having a dream with my eyes wide open and not realizing it was only a dream. Time and space were nonexistent. I felt I was in the future, for what I was feeling was not known to me from my past. There was no sense of good or bad, for logically how could I know if it were good or bad. I was never there before and I had never felt like this. I didn't know whether or not to fight this intruder that had entered my space uninvited. But how does one resist a feeling? It is like trying to fight a wisp of air? This emotion had brought with it a new and different feeling, but into my being it was. Was it a dream?

When I realized that what I felt was being caused by only a dream, the realization of that fact was worse than the dream. I was afraid that in reality I would lose what I felt in the dream. I began to detest the transition from the unreal to the real world while at the same time being forced to accept the change. My intellect made me accept that what had happened was only a dream. The realization that it was only a dream was the cruelest reality to have to accept. The control is gone. The real world is all too real. The present is now and what was has passed. To deny that fact is wistful. To live in the dream world is much nicer except the dream has its own master, for no one can control a dream.

The reality that you're an occasional visitor and not the master of your faith is what causes the fear. For one may sleep upon command but a different power must supply the dream. As the outsider I had no choice but to wait until the dream reappeared. I tried to rationalize what I was feeling. After eliminating all the things I had experienced before I had to find some new words for what I was feeling now.

As I tried to analyze the grip that the dream had on me I felt a fear come over me as I left the real world. I was daring to venture into my mind rather than using my mind to find the problem. I finally realized that the answer was not in my mind. I had no experience in emotions, but I did not realize that until that very moment. Reacting to tangible things created my life's experiences and here I was being confronted by an intangible. My emotions had been tucked away and I did not even know it. Love and fear were not the type of things I ever dealt with before.

When I saw Betsy, I knew it wasn't hate, so that only left love. That word I had not heard for a long time and could not remember when I ever used it. I was infuriated at myself for realizing this late in my life that such an emotion existed and this was the first time I felt it. It had to be in a dream. But was it a dream? For if it was, it was a fabulous dream. But why was I in fear. My fist clenched so tightly that I drove my nail into my palm again. The sharp pain distracted me, but not for long. My mouth was so dry I could not speak or swallow. Was I to conclude that what I was feeling was genuinely the emotion of love? For what else could it be? At that point I gave up and was happy in the fact that whatever it was, I enjoyed it and let it go at that. I was no longer in fear that the feeling would not come again. I vowed that I would be ready next time. I left the porch and went to the shore to get my sandals. Just seeing them made me tremble, for I had to ask myself was it just a dream?

The rest of the day I went sightseeing in the area. I visited the small churches and little shops in town. I decided to try a restaurant in town rather than risking another feast with the hotel manager. The day and night seemed to melt into one. That night the previous night's intruder did not revisit me so my only companion was sleep.

The next day I drove to the Vatican, not to the business offices where I had been before when I had done some work for the church but to Saint Peter's itself. I tried to get permission to see the Pope, but all the people who could arrange such a meeting that I had met from previous trips had been reassigned or else retired. I started to feel ridiculous. I asked myself, "What could he do?"

I walked around the inside of St. Peter's Church seeking some sort of logical answer for what I perceived had happened to me, and forgiveness, but I didn't know for what. These dreams or visions were not a vision of some lustful desire and in fact, I couldn't even understand myself why these thoughts were starting to consistently plague me. I found a quiet corner of the church and sat down. I began looking around the church as though I was expecting to find some sign or anything to help explain what I was experiencing. I started to feel as though all the icons were looking at me, rather than me looking at them. Religion had never been a strong point with me, but to now find myself in a church...looking for an answer to a problem that I couldn't even define, started to unnerve me even more. I started to question myself as to what I was doing sitting in church miles from home. I began to tremble. I found myself getting infuriated at myself for trembling.

"Sir, are you all right?"

I heard this voice and I stopped breathing.

"Sir, are you alright?"

I heard it again, but I still paid the speaker no mind as I started to walk out of the church. My curiosity got the better of me and I turned to see where the words came from. I was astonished as I looked at a little old man, bent over with age, desperately leaning on his cane. He had to keep moving the cane from side to side to maintain his balance. He was practically bald and his skin wrinkled with a pale ash white color. His clothes were an assortment of color and style, put on only to clothe him. His voice had cracked under the strain of speaking and it was obvious to me that speaking was down with extreme difficulty. The pathetic sight only intensified my own anger at myself. As tears started to well in my eyes, I had to turn away. My anger was quickly turning into another emotion, but I couldn't describe it, only that it made me feel mad while at the same time, sorry for me. As I turned again to look at this old man...trembling, as he was...I just walked over to him and kissed him on his balding head and pushed some money into his torn jacket pocket.

"I'm all right...I'll make...you take care of you." I pressed some more money into his hand, turned and left the church, but more resolved in my own mind that I could overcome anything, this problem or whatever it is, is no different. I also knew that there were no answers for me in Italy.

The old man walked after me and tried to give the money back. I stopped, for I was afraid he would fall. When he got next to me he grabbed the sleeve of my jacket to balance himself. I said, "No, please, you keep it. Please" My words, sounded more like a pray than a command.

The old man put the money in his pants pocket, but again grabbed my sleeve as he said, "Come, come, my friend Cardinal Carmine, he can help."

I looked at the old man, irritated at myself for even listening to him. I was more annoyed because I was following him as he held on to my sleeve and we walked out one of the side entrances of Saint Peter's Church. A Swiss guard came over to us, but my guide said something and we were allowed to pass through the gate that led to a side yard of the St. Peters complex. A guard station became our next obstacle but, again, a few words from the old man, and I was shown a bench to sit on.

"Where are we going?" I asked as I complied with the guard's request to have a seat.

The old man kept saying, "You'll see, you'll see. Sit...they come."

Within a few moments a young man came from one of the buildings and spoke to the guard. Next, there was a discussion between the guards, the old man and the young novice. At the end of the discussion the young man came over to me and in perfect English said, "Please excuse the secrecy, but the new security system they have installed has made all of us become more aware of what is happening in the world. Come with me, your friend has asked for and has been granted a meeting for you with Cardinal Carmine. The Cardinal is in the garden, but if you follow me I will show you the way."

I looked at the young man in disbelief. The only word that I could say was "Why?" I followed the young novice as he quickened his pace as he walked through the maze of buildings that surround St. Peters. I was following, but all of a sudden I stopped. "Wait." My command startled the young man as he almost fell as he tried to stop and turn to face me all at the same time. He looked at me not knowing what to expect. As he looked like a little boy who was caught with his hands in the cookie tin. "Before we go any further I would like to know what is going on and where are we going?"

The novice got a look of astonishment on his face. He stared at me for a moment before he said, "I am taking you to see Cardinal Carmine. Isn't that what you wanted? I was called by the Cardinal to go and fetch you."

"I don't know this Cardinal. I just met that old man in the church and the next thing I know I am here with you." As I spoke I could feel the anger in me increase.

"That old man you referring to was the Cardinal's private guard. He was assigned to the Cardinal the day Cardinal Carmine became Cardinal. That old man as you keep referring to him saved the Cardinal's life by pushing the Cardinal out of the way of an assassin's bullet and fighting off two others until help came."

"I'm referring to him as an old man since I didn't know his name, not to be disrespectful. I just met him in the church." I was visibly embarrassed for what I said since I felt my face redden from my comment.

"Well you must have said something. He has asked the Cardinal to see you and the Cardinal agreed. He usual spends this part of the day in meditation. Because of that old man, he is interrupting his normal schedule to see you. Now I think you should follow me so we don't keeping him waiting too long." The novice turned and continued his ever-increasing pace until we were in a little courtyard. The novice motioned for me to wait as he approached the Cardinal who was walking around the courtyard with his head bowed. The courtyard was in the middle of a square of buildings. Each building had a balcony and at least two doors that opened out into the courtyard. There were walkways that crisscrossed the yard with the always-present fountain in the middle. The flowers and vines that were everywhere were starting to show the effects of the onslaught of winter. The bright coloration of autumn was starting to show on some of the plants. The entire setting was one that spoke of solitude and tranquility. If ever I were in a place to meditate this certainly was it. I could not hear my footsteps as I walked around. I was so engrossed in my thoughts and inspection of the courtyard that I didn't take notice of the Cardinal standing right next to me. When I turned my head to look at more of my surroundings I was startled to come face to face with him. We were the same height and build. Looking at him was like looking in a mirror. Our hair was the same color as were the rest of our features. A warm smile came across his face as he extended his hand to shake hands with me.

"My good friend, or the Old Man as you refer to him, has asked me to see you because he says you are carrying a great burden that I might lighten for you or at least help you to carry. My novice has told me he told you of my affection for the Old Man so that just leaves us to discuss what is troubling you so much that he would feel you need my help."

As the Cardinal spoke, he casually walked down one of the walkways and I found myself walking with him. His voice had a soothing quality about it that put me right at ease. In the few moments that I had met him I felt that I had known him all of my life. My own stubbornness made me curious to speak to this stranger. Cardinal or not, I didn't know him and why should I tell him anything. What could he do about me thinking I was going crazy? I had just seen something on the beach and this guy wasn't there. I didn't know him. It was none of his darn business. I wasn't some little kid being told to go confess my sins to some stranger. I was walking next to him only because I didn't want to be rude, not because I needed him. That old man should have minded his own business. I kept questioning myself what I was doing in the courtyard and with the people around me. The young man, the Cardinal's novice, just made me nervous and I didn't know why. What the hell was he all about? Anyway, how did he learn to speak English so well? He certainly didn't learn from the Cardinal. The Cardinal sounded like some greenhorn back home. Home, that's where I should be going.

"My novice was born in your country and was educated in New Jersey. He wastes too much of his time trying to improve my English." The words the Cardinal said made my mind go blank.

The Cardinal continued, "But we are not here to talk about me. I realize you are reluctant to discuss your personal matters with a stranger, but you have to talk to someone that is very obvious, so why not to me. I have heard many stories before and even if I can't help sometimes just saying the words out loud creates the basis for better understanding the problem yourself. Here, let me help you get started. I came to Italy to…?"

I was so infuriated by this guy coming into my space that I was void of any ability to answer. Or so I thought. What I said was, "To meet with some people to see if they could help me with a problem I am having in New Jersey. After I was done with my business I decided to take a few days off and my hotel clerk in Salerno recommended a resort that the locals use." I continued to tell the Cardinal about the hotel and the sighting I had of Betsy. He listened very intently as he kept a steady pace as we walked around and around the garden. I ended the story with, "I'm sorry I am taking up so much of your time."

The Cardinal looked at me as a wisp of a smile came across his face as he responded, "I always have time to help people understand things they have a hard time understanding by themselves. If you had seen Christ we would be calling it a miracle. The fact that you saw someone else doesn't make it any less of a miracle to you. You had an experience that you are trying to understand and you can't make sense of it. Not everything can be described by using conventional terms. The battle between our intellect and our emotions is always an ongoing battle. Your problem is that you have to call upon a different part of your being, one you don't understand and have no experience in using. When someone reports to the church that they have witnessed a sighting there are two questions that are asked. The answer to these two questions may give you your answer. You understand, of course, you will never find a simple answer but rather bit-by-bit you will accept what happened to you as being just another one of life's mysteries. The first thing you have to do is tell me why you were at that place at this time of your life, and secondly, why there? Why not some other places? Was this the first time you ever saw this person? It is knowing what started the chain of events as well as the chain of events that will start to give you a better insight as to what happened and why at this time it did happen. You must have thought of these things yourself? So start with 'one morning I...'"

"You understand a lot of what I'm going to say is not always based upon my own experiences, but rather the results of reasoning and hearsay?"

"Only an attorney would use a word like 'hearsay.' Are you an attorney?"

I laughed and replied, "Yes. Where do I start my story?"

"Well, that's all right, I'm not a jury and start as far back as you can." The Cardinal hesitated in our walk and in our conversation. It was as though he were collecting his strength to continue walking and to collect his thoughts to continue talking.

After a few minutes he started, "One morning…now, you continue."

# Chapter Two

The phone rang in my office and was answered by my machine. After the fourth ring, the machine picked up: "You have reached the office of George. I am temporarily out of the office. Please leave your name and phone number and I shall return your call as soon as I return." The only response the caller gave was to hang up. When I got to the office later that morning at 10, the call was repeated:

"George." I answered.

"George." Came the reply

"Yes." I said.

"I would like to make an appointment to see you. I had called earlier, but your machine answered and I didn't want to leave a message." The caller responded.

"What about?"

"Where?"

"When?"

I fired the questions into the phone without really thinking about them.

"My car will pick you up today about ten o'clock; will that be all right?"

The caller continued talking with a sound of urgency in his voice, "I'd rather not go into any great detail over the phone at this time however, you can be assured you will be compensated for your time."

"Sir, I don't know who you are, you sound sincere, but no way am I going for a ride with someone I don't know." I sat there waiting for a response.

The unidentified voice hesitated and finally continued: "I would rather not come to your office, but I guess you are right. I must sound strange but I assure you I am not."

"Okay, listen," I said. "We'll meet for lunch. Do you know where Ferry Street is in Newark?"

"Yes." The unidentified caller responded.

"Well, off Ferry, the block next to Monroe, there is a restaurant called Rio Limo. I'll meet you there at one o'clock," I told him, still rather annoyed at myself for going.

"Okay, when you see me you'll remember me." The caller responded.

"Don't worry about it. We will probably be the only two people in the place. I'll see you at that time," I said as I hung up the phone.

After the call I racked my memory as to where I had heard the voice before. I knew I had, but for the life of me I could not remember. About 12:30 p.m., I buttoned up my vest, put on my jacket and left. It was a little windy and brisk out as I hurried to get in the car and drive to the restaurant. As usual, there were no parking spaces, but this time I wasn't too mad since my curiosity got the better of me. I wanted to see whether or not I would recognize any car that would pull up. None came.

I finally found a place to park and at one o'clock in the afternoon I went into the bar section of the restaurant. I peered into the back room. The back room of the Rio Limo was about 30-feet-wide by 50-feet-long. There were tables evenly spaced throughout the entire room except for an aisle left open to the kitchen. The tables were set for four people with a white tablecloth and green napkins. There was a knife, fork and spoon by each dish and a vase with a fake rose in the center of the table. Except for the path to the kitchen it was difficult to move through the room, as I had to dodge the tables and chairs.

The walls were decorated with painted scenes. The scenes were depicting some sort of combination of ships, harbors and ocean. The ceiling was painted a dull white and the room was dimly lit. There were no windows in the room, which made it look even smaller. At the far end of room there was a little stage, but the tables were pressed right up against it. As I looked around the room, it took a few seconds for my eyes to focus on the only customer.

I was shocked. I had only met the man once and for only a brief period of time. It was Mr. Fields, the president of the third largest drug firm in the United States. They had just built a large office and laboratory complex in Woodbridge, New Jersey, and expanded its physical plant in Bloomfield three-fold. I had met Mr. Fields about six months earlier. He was 50-years-old about 6-feet-tall with dyed brown hair except around the temples where it was gray. He weighed about 170 pounds, but was not muscular. His manicured, polished nails flashed even in the poorly lit back room of the restaurant. His eyebrows were very thin which gave his long face a feminine look. He was dressed in a dark blue suit with a white shirt and a dark blue tie. The exact same outfit he had worn the last time I had seen him. Somehow, he looked a lot older now; his eyes had bags under them, which made him look as though he hadn't slept all night. No matter how hard I tried to concentrate on him, or even begin to go through all the reasons why he would call me, I kept thinking about his wife and the circumstances that surrounded the meeting. The last time I had seen him, he was with his wife who was a little shorter than him. It was his second marriage. She was 35-years-old, slightly built, and weighed about 120 pounds. Her brown hair glistened as though it had little lights in it and her big eyes seemed to look right through you. She moved about almost effortlessly as though she were skating. She wore very little make-up and only clear-colored nail polish. She was the type of person who you would not call beautiful, but you were struck by her overall appearance. The only problem with her was when she spoke her voice was in complete contrast to her physical appearance. She had the type of voice that was very shrill and piercing, she left the listener with the feeling that he was listening to some unrefined street walker rather than the wife of one of the most influential men in the drug industry. The contrast between the Mr. and Mrs. Fields was even more pronounced when the two were viewed in contrast to each other.

The house the Fields lived in was an old estate in Princeton, New Jersey. There was a main house with two smaller buildings off to the side. One of the smaller buildings was left vacant while the other had been connected from a carriage house to a garage with a four-room apartment upstairs, which was used by the servants. The main house had three floors. On the first floor was a large entranceway with stairs leading to the upper floors. Off the entrance way was four doors, one led to an enormous dining room, the second to a living room, the third to a library and the fourth to a hallway that led back to a large patio which had a door from each of the rooms, except the kitchen, opening onto it.

The second floor had five bedroom suites with their own bathrooms attached and the cook and chauffeur divided the third floor into two apartments that were currently being used. Because of the size of the house the Fields regularly employed four domestics: a chauffeur, maid, butler and cook.

During the criminal trial the testimony was that their butler and maid had quit because of a fight they had with Mrs. Fields. Mrs. Fields had a sister in England who was in the employment business; she hired maids and butlers for Americans. Mrs. Fields had called her sister in London and told her to find replacements for them.

The sister had found a young couple for the Fields. She called Mrs. Fields to come to England to interview the couple; their names were John and Lynn. That was when Mrs. Fields first met the young couple who were to become my clients.

They weren't married, but they posed as a married couple since they felt it would be easier to obtain employment as a maid-butler/cook combination. Mrs. Fields went to England, interviewed and hired them and brought them into the U.S. on a visitor's visas, promising them green cards within six months. For a person to work in the United States, they must have a job and/or promise of employment and have skills that are not readily available in this country. Once these requirements are met, the worker is given a work permit. The permit is printed on "green cards" hence the expression "green card" had become known to all who wish to work in the United States. To an immigrant, the mere promise of obtaining a green card is a "dream come true" since they are very hard to obtain. A visa is granted to anyone who wishes to visit a country, but to get a green card is an achievement in and of itself.

When John and Lynn arrived, they were given the apartment over the garage to live in. Their duties were written up in the same manner as a job description would be written for an office worker. It was very obvious to them that their new employer had a "professional" come in and write up the various duties of the domestics. Right from the first day, Lynn and Mrs. Fields didn't get along. No matter what the job, Lynn didn't do it properly. No matter what was said, Mrs. Fields would snap at Lynn in a cruel, almost savage, outburst. Lynn would quietly take it for fear of not getting a green card as promised. John tried to keep the two separated, but try as he may; it seemed the two would come together. After three months, Lynn begged John to quit. She just couldn't take it any longer. Mrs. Fields would never miss an opportunity to pass a snide remark about Lynn both personally and professionally.

John thought it would be a good idea if Lynn and he got away to the Pocono's for a weekend. While they were there, Lynn again begged John to look for other employment. She confessed that she had registered their names with agencies in California and New York. She had read advertisements in the paper and responded to them. At first John was infuriated but he realized that something had to give so he promised to go along with Lynn's plans.

When they came back to the house from their weekend, it was like a demon had been turned loose and took on the shape of Mrs. Fields. Her outbursts became more frequent and cutting. Lynn was at her wits end to contain herself. By now they were in the United States for three months and Mrs. Fields never mentioned anything about getting them their green cards. Lynn asked John to ask about it and, after much persuasion, he finally got up enough nerve to bring the topic up to Mr. Fields who, up to now, had kept his contact with them to an absolute minimum. He flatly refused to get involved and told John that any dealings would have to be made with Mrs. Fields. This infuriated Lynn even more.

She wanted to leave immediately, but John, in his smooth, becoming way, convinced her to stay at least until they had enough saved to get back to England. Lynn agreed, but the next morning Lynn called an employment agency that she had listed their names with, and was shocked to hear that the agency had written to her twice about a job in California, house sitting for a movie director while he was on location shooting a film.

That night while Lynn was serving dinner, she overheard the Fields discussing their trip to Paris. She couldn't believe it, so she asked Mrs. Fields if John and she could have the week off, without pay, of course, to take a trip also. Mrs. Fields said she would let them know, but Mr. Fields surprised Lynn by interrupting his wife and told Lynn it would be all right. At first, John didn't believe Lynn but Mr. Fields confirmed that they could have the week off the following morning as he was leaving for the office. (He also pressed two 100 dollar bills into John's jacket pocket.) Lynn called a travel agent and booked a flight to California for the next week when the Fields were going to Paris.

John and Lynn went to California for a week to be interviewed by the agency and their potential employer. While they were there, they did some sightseeing. The week flew by, and they boarded the plane for the flight home. As they were leaving the plane, the FBI arrested them in Kennedy airport. They were transported to Princeton, New Jersey that day.

While they were gone, the Fields had returned and upon their arrival Mrs. Fields filed a criminal complaint against them for stealing a fur coat and jewelry valued at $100.000.00; a car valued at $10,000.00 and forging her name to a check for $500.00.

Upon their arrival in Princeton, New Jersey, where the Fields live, they were arraigned. Lynn and John knew only one couple in America, and were able to convince a judge that they were innocent and should be released without bail. The judge, who heard their bail plea, belonged to the same country club as the Fields and had heard many stories about Mr. Fields' second wife and her erratic behavior when it came to the "domestics." The judge ordered that John and Lynn would have to surrender their visas to the police. He asked them where they would go. John and Lynn explained that while they were in California they had met a couple from Long Island and asked to call them. They told them of their plight and instead of the couple just hanging up, they vouched for John and Lynn and the judge ordered their release. When news of this reached Mrs. Fields she became enraged to the point that she started to throw things about the house. She called her husband at work and insisted that he intercede. He tried but the judge would not be swayed and the defendants were released without bail.

Upon arriving in Long Island, John and Lynn begged their friends for guidance and help as to what they should do. They had no money, no place to go, but swore they were innocent. The people they were staying with had a friend Russ, who knew everything and everybody. After a series of phone calls, Russ called me. I was going to get John and Lynn out of the country but the charges of theft and forgery would still be on their records. The charges could only be explained away by a "not guilty" verdict. I represented them in the criminal trial and they were found "not guilty." The charges and trial were still on John and Lynn's record. For this reason, I felt that the record of the arrest would greatly affect their ability to get work as domestics. I felt that the charges although proven not to be true would have to be explained. The only way for John and Lynn to be vindicated would be to sue the Fields for malicious prosecution. I was in the process of starting a malicious prosecution suit against the Fields when I received the phone call.

As I approached Mr. Fields, I couldn't help but smile; I knew that he knew I was going to sue him but to have him give up so easily! What to settle for, that was the question? As I sat down, he half-raised out of his chair to greet me, but I could see he didn't really even know I was there.

After a long hesitation he finally looked up and said, "George, it was nice of you to come on such short notice, I appreciate it. I really do want to talk to you."

"Mr. Fields, I don't think it is proper for me to meet with you since you must know I represent John and Lynn and I am going to sue you. Without your attorney being here, I really don't think I can discuss the case with you, and I must tell you that the raw deal those kids got from your wife has not made me one of your admirers."

"George, I assure you that we will not discuss that case. I also assure you that the situation with John and Lynn will be settled to your satisfaction, but that's not why I'm here," he said.

"Well sir, going on the assumption I'm not good looking, why? Wait, here comes the waiter. Let's put in our order. He knows what I want. I come here often; what would you like?" I asked.

"Just double whatever you're having," he said.

24

"How about wine?"

"Okay."

The waiter nodded and scurried off to get the order.

"Now Mr. Fields, what do you want from me and why?"

"George, since we will be working together, I think we should drop the formalities. I'm going to tell you a story, an incredible one, but a story all the same. I have to rely upon your professionalism not to repeat it."

"Mr. Fields, I don't know your first name, nor do I care to. Before you tell me any stories, I better tell you about the two signs in my office; they are hand painted on scrolls, framed, and hung on the wall for all to see. They are in Italian since I don't know Latin. One says, tell me what you will give—I know what you want. And the other..."

At this point Mr. Fields changed color, obviously annoyed. He slid back into the chair and said, "The other reads, 'Ass, gas or grass—no one does nothing for nothing.' I assure you I know of your signs; I know of your demented analogy of an attorney and a whore, and I even know of your only friend. I didn't get to where I am by not being prepared or by not having done my homework. I have, in my pocket, two checks, one for ten thousand and one thousand. The ten thousand is a retainer and the one thousand for your silence if we can't make a deal."

"Listen! I don't know why you got me here but you play your trumpet again—well just don't. If you want my help, relax; I'll solve your problem. But first, why am I here? Why me? That's the part that I don't understand." Before I could finish, Mr. Fields interrupted.

"George, I did some research on you, and the consensus was that you're an old fashioned mercenary caught up in modern times. That's what I need for this matter. Also, your handling of the John and Lynn's case impressed me. As you know, I exert some influence. To get the FBI to make an arrest on a citizen's complaint takes some doing, especially when you know your wife is like mine…well you know what I mean…your handling of the trial was, I thought, brilliant and to get the jury to return a verdict in less than fifteen minutes after a six day trial…well, I was impressed. I got a transcript of the trial and sent it to our dear attorneys who saw that I was greatly impressed, especially since you were on a limited budget. I can appreciate ability when I see it. Also, very few people know you and I can't use the normal channels opened to me to solve my problem, does that satisfy you?" I nodded my head and he continued.

"George, assume for the moment a person came to you and told you that their father, husband, child or whoever had taken a pill and died. The doctor, upon examining the body, discovered a poison, and by conducting a certain test could trace the poison to a pill he had just taken. Also, the doctor could get two other experts to back him up. What would you do?"

"I'd find out the manufacturer of the pill and who sold it to him, and sue the bastard. Why do you ask?"

"How would you know who to sue?"

"What difference does it make? I'd sue everyone!"

"What if I told you such an incident did happen and it could bankrupt my company?" Fields asked as he became visibly more nervous.

"My response would be; 'Wait, here comes the waiter, let's eat first.'" I said.

"George, your attention span seems to last about ten minutes. It goes from money to food."

"Well, Mr. Fields, I didn't realize that you were perfect. I'll try to be also," I answered.

"Your point is well taken George." The waiter, recognizing that his presence was not wanted, hurried and put the food and wine down and left.

"The fact that your company would be bankrupt would only get me to move quicker," I said. "I would want my case settled while you still have money." My answer annoyed him.

"Exactly, the cost of pre-trial discovery would be in the millions without even trying to put a dollar value on the jury awards." By now Mr. Fields had started to sweat even though the room was cool. As he was speaking, he kept playing with the silverware and dish. Throughout the conversation he kept staring at the table as though he were reading a script. It was as though I wasn't even sitting there and he was reciting a story he wrote.

"Well, how can I help? Damn! I spilled the gravy on my shirt," I said as I tried to dry it with the napkin.

"George, you had better finish your lunch before dealing with my problem." Mr. Fields was visibly upset.

"Mr. Fields, that's twice; I can understand your nervousness, that's to be expected, but if I can be of any help to you, you have to relax. I understand what you want; time is of the essence and the stakes are high. I just don't have the answers up my sleeve."

"George, I don't think you understand the problem!"

"Well, let me tell you what I think it is, okay? You want, rather need, a story or reason why people would take your pill and die. The story will have to be one that people will believe for a cost less than defending such a suit, right!"

At first Mr. Fields couldn't speak. He looked in disbelief. His facial expression revealed that I had hit upon the problem. At the same time it showed a tremendous feeling of security that he had chosen the right man.

He put down the spoon he had been playing with, sat up in the chair, and looked me right in the eye. "Exactly," he finally was able to say, "Exactly." He shook my hand as a further indication of his confidence in me.

"See, I told you I knew it; let us now discuss what is in it for me? How much of a budget do I have to spend in order to achieve the results you want?"

Mr. Fields just stiffened up in the chair. He tried not to show his furor but that failed as he said, "How do I get your mind off money...don't you realize what's at stake here...can you be that callous? But why shouldn't you be, it's my problem not yours. If I give you a number, it'll be too low. I should have never told you that it would cost millions. That was stupid."

"Sir, if you don't think I already know that you have gotten the wrong man. Get help from someone else. Your own firm's attorney's rates are astronomical and all they do is write letters or sit in court with a bunch of other overpriced attorneys." As I was speaking, Fields was squirming in the chair. It was obvious he was not used to having anyone speak to him the way I was. One good thing did come of it; Fields had calmed down a lot.

"George, I will pay you in stages: Namely, so much to come up with an idea, so much to implement it, so much to achieve it and an annuity in terms of an employment contract for life." He said the phase as though he had recited it many times.

"I hear what you are saying," I replied. "However, I am more interested in specific amounts rather than abstract concepts."

Mr. Fields continued. "To start with, I told you I have two checks in my pocket; they should get you started." He handed me the checks and a piece of paper. "Here is my private number; you can talk to me and only me, directly. When will I hear from you? I must move on this immediately."

I looked at the checks and the piece of paper with the phone number on it and said, "I will call you, not tomorrow but the next day, at one o'clock, give me at least a day, okay?"

"Okay," he responded. "Good-bye." He turned abruptly and left.

As Mr. Fields was leaving, I started to wonder whether or not I had done the right thing. I was to find out later that he had hired a female detective a week earlier to check me out and she couldn't find any reason not to hire me. I finally resolved that he had decided he had to trust someone so why not me? I followed him as he left the restaurant as he walked two blocks to a car that looked like he had taken it from the car pool. He got in it and drove away.

After Mr. Fields left, I returned to the restaurant and finished my lunch. After lunch I just sat there trying to comprehend what had happened. I couldn't help feeling proud. Of all the people Fields could call on, he had hired me, but why hire me? So he was impressed. I concluded that for whatever the reason, he made his own decision! I fingered the two checks and wondered if I should rush to cash them before he changed his mind. I paid the bill and left.

"Was she involved in your work at this time?" The Cardinal's question came as a surprise to me. I wasn't sure he was listening and here he was asking questions. "She didn't work for you?" His questions were having the same effect as a person slapping me. Each question hurt and made me feel more uncomfortable. He was questioning me. He was in my mind with me. That thought infuriated me more than the one before. I could feel the anger in me start to swell. The words I said were, "No. I didn't work with her. I was starting to tell you the chain of events that brought me to Salerno, Italy at that time. I was starting from the beginning."

His warm smile disarmed me again and he said, "That is good. The more you remember, the better prepared you will be to comprehend what happened. Continue. I am sorry I interrupted it's just that I wanted to get a better understanding of what was happening to you and why. Please continue, but keep in mind the problem facing you is not unlike the problems you solve for other people. They hire you to clean up their messes and here you are with your own to do. Alas/alack my son, both problems have at their root the same six masters who, what, why, where, how and when. Your problem is easier. The 'who' is you. What is a vision? Where is Italy? When is now? The only answers you are looking for are how and why. The how

29

you fear may be divine intervention or just some physical reason. For the why you must start from where you are starting, the very beginning. Please continue, I am sorry I interrupted you." The Cardinal raised his hand and within a few moments juice was served to us in the courtyard. We sat at a little table to enjoy it. When we were done I continued telling my story.

# Chapter Three

When I got back to my office, I started to prepare an outline for the case. Thinking logically is great since it doesn't require any moral or ethical decisions. There are no judgmental decisions. Black or white, that is all that is needed. Generally speaking, all problems have not a best answer but rather an answer that is least bad. Surely this problem could be anticipated in the same fashion. What was the problem? What caused it? What were the possible solutions? Which would I choose? Why?

The problem, the way I saw it, was dollars and cents. Product liability, that's what Fields was worried about. I dialed a fellow attorney, Harry.

"Hello Harry, this is George."

Harry responded in his usual low monotone. Harry was an attorney I had met some years back and with whom I had collaborated in a few cases. He had worked for a firm that specialized in defending lawsuits for insurance companies. He, if anyone, would know the approximate cost of defending a lawsuit of this magnitude.

"Harry, I have a client whose husband took some sort of drug and she thinks it killed him."

"How old was he?"

"About forty."

"What did he do?"

"He was a carpenter."

"How does she know the pill killed him?"

"She doesn't."

"Do you have a doctor's report? If not, don't worry about it. I can get one for you."

"Not yet, but assuming the pill did kill him, how do I prove it and what sort of damages am I looking for?"

"Well George, his productive life was twenty-five years; twenty-five times twenty-five thousand would be damages of at least six hundred and twenty-five thousand plus with inflation, etc. It would depend on how strong a case you could develop for negligence. Well, you can examine their people and serve them interrogatories to find out what happened. Even if you lose, it will still cost them a small fortune to defend, so move fast before someone else does."

"Well Harry, let me see if I get the case. I'll call you back, okay?"

"Yeah. I'll see you."

"Good-bye."

After I hung up the phone, I realized, for the first time, the type of case I was dealing with. No wonder Mr. Fields was so upset, this was negligence. It wasn't like the Johns Manville case where the government would be issuing reports.

I pulled out an old file in which I kept newspaper clippings on cases that interested me. One of them involved an asbestos manufacturer. The government had run tests to see why so many people, who were working in the plant, were getting cancer and they traced it to the asbestos that was in the air. Based on that, everyone who worked there or who had installed the insulation sued the company immediately. The cost of the suits bankrupted the company. This case would be decided on a case-by-case basis, which would defer the cost over a number of years and greatly increase the cost of handling it. The phone rang, I picked it up and it was Harry again.

"George?"

"Yes?"

"I was just thinking your suit would start against the store where the lady's husband purchased the pills. The store would have a cause of action against the manufacturer and so would your client."

"Why is that?" I asked.

"Well, your client would have to sue the person they dealt with since her husband had nothing to do with the manufacturer."

"Okay, Harry, thanks."

"Good-bye."

After I hung up with Harry, I began to estimate what cases like this one was worth. Harry seemed very excited and his eagerness to help only strengthened my feeling that cases involving product liability were worth big money. Harry had a sixth sense when it came to solving a case. Again the phone rang, but it was just a wrong number. I left the office and put the whole matter out of my mind. I resolved that the morning would be a better time to start working on a new case.

In the morning, I went to the library to look up some of the product liability type cases from all over the country, in order to sound somewhat knowledgeable when I discussed the case again with Mr. Fields. I still had the two checks in my pocket and decided to cash them before he stopped payment on them since I still did not understand why he had come to me. When I got to the bank, the line was right out the door so I decided not to wait. I left and proceeded downtown to the library. When I finally got to the library, the place was mobbed. I had forgotten that just before the holidays everyone would be studying for mid-term exams, so I left.

I still had the checks, and no matter how I tried, I could not shake the idea that Mr. Fields might stop payment on them, so I drove back to the bank, waited in the line, and tried to cash them. It was just dumb luck that the checks were drawn on the same bank my account was in. When I got inside the bank and gave my check to the teller she called over the manager.

"George," the manager said.

"Yes."

"You know that if we give you ten thousand in cash, we

have to send a special report to the IRS."

"I didn't know that."

"Well, we do." She replied with a smile she reserved for those occasions when she knew she was saying something I didn't know and I didn't want to hear.

"Well, give me back the check for ten thousand and just cash the one for a thousand."

"Okay," she said.

I got the money for the one check and kept the other. I left and went to my office. As I was entering, the phone rang.

"Hello, George?" It was Harry.

"George?" He half shouted.

"Yes."

"Is it possible the druggist screwed up rather than the manufacturer?"

"I don't know."

"Well, it's something to think about, because if he did, your suit would only be against the store and your case wouldn't be worth as much."

"Why not?" I asked.

"A jury will feel sorry for an independent store owner more than a big company!" he snapped back.

"Yeah, I guess you're right. Well, thanks for calling." I said.

I hung up and vowed that if he called again, I would just hang up. Harry was the kind of person who never quit...he would get an idea and go on and on about it until you agreed with him or you just agreed to shut him up. What he said made sense. If we could somehow get the individual stores to take the blame, that would surely reduce the cost to the company. That was definitely a possibility. There was one thing for sure; the company's name had to be left out of the case, but how? Trying to put the blame on the individual stores would involve many different people and each of them would have to be schooled on what to say. Each of them would have to keep their mouth shut…and how legal is that…was there a legal answer? If there were a legal answer, would that answer bankrupt the company and what about involvement? I was being asked to do something that might put me in the position of playing God, Judge and Jury… who was I to decide whether or not this company should exist? What about the people who died and their families? They would have to be compensated for their loss…there, that's one part of the problem solved, the company's name would have to be left out of it. Someone, somewhere, someday would have to make decisions, so why not me here and now. There were different groups to be considered: the victims and their families; the stockholders of the company; the people they employed; the creditors of the company and me. What about me? There are dollars and cents involved; the moral issue as well as the possible legal problems and I'll have to get enough to retire on because if the truth comes out, who knows what will happen. I'll need to overpay everyone or else no one will want to get involved. I went home and kept going over all of the elements of the case. As each thought came to mind it acted as a stimulus for the next idea…that set up a chain reaction…all of which kept me awake long into the dark night. I finally got up and sat in my chair in the living room and read the paper.

There was a production of the play Jane Eyre at a local theater and a friend of mine called an invited me to go, but I decided to stay home.

The name stuck in my mind, but I didn't know why. It was something I remembered, but didn't know what it was. One good thing about it, it got my mind off the case and I fell asleep thinking of Jane Eyre.

The Cardinal got up and I thought he wanted me to leave, so I got up as well. "No. Sit and continue. I had wine and fruit bought." The Cardinal dismissed the servant as he undertook to pour the wine and serve the fruit.

# Chapter Four

The next morning I was still tired because all night I had tried working the problem every which way, but the one main thought was the same. Somehow the attention would have to be diverted from the company to the individual stores or to anyone else since a jury would go easier on them. The Jane Eyre thing just left my mind. Before I knew it, it was one o'clock, time to call Mr. Fields. According to the area code the number he had given me was located in New York City. I dialed it and Mr. Fields answered, "Hello."

"Mr. Fields, this is George."

"Yes."

"It is in my New York apartment."

"That's nice."

"Do you have any suggestions as to the answer to the problem we discussed? Where do you want to meet?" He said with an annoyed tone.

"Meet me in the same place in Newark at six o'clock, okay? And bring ten thousand in small bills with you," I added.

That night at 6 p.m., I walked in and there was Mr. Fields, still with a bewildered look on his face, but calmer as he sat there slowly fingering the silverware as though he were polishing it. I sat down and he looked up and he greeted me by nodding his head.

"Well, have you an answer, or are you here to return the ten thousand dollar check since you have already cashed the thousand dollar one?"

"You sure get your information fast, but I didn't come here to argue with you. I came here to get an agreement as to my fee and also to find out how, specifically, poison got into your company's pills."

"George, I didn't mean to antagonize you, it's just that, well you know, aside from my own personal fortune, do you have any idea the effect that this problem would have on the market place if word got out. The millions of shareholders who would get hurt, the small people who would be destroyed, the…"

"Wait a minute, before you go into the second chorus of God Bless America, just answer my question. How did the poison get into the pills?"

"Do you know anything about chemistry?"

"No."

"Well, you can have chemical A and chemical B, both of which are good. To make the drug last longer, you add a third drug, chemical C. Now, A and C or B and C are in certain ratios. A, B and C are good for you or at best, won't hurt you if measured correctly, however, this same combination, A, B, C mixture raised to two hundred degrees, produces cyanide poison. We had such a mixture and somehow it was placed inside the drying ovens prematurely or left in too long, we don't know which. This mixture turned to poison. The individual pills were disbursed into packets and some of them, approximately fifty, were shipped out."

"Do you mean fifty packets?"

"No, just fifty pills. We caught the mistake, but one section of pills, fifty to a tray, got past the quality control and were mixed into the normal floor of goods, and shipped out."

"Can we localize where?"

"No, they were shipped out all over the U.S."

"Is it possible that all fifty pills are in one packet?"

"Yes, but I doubt it, since the odds of that happening are extremely high."

"What about calling the entire batch back?"

"Do you have any idea what that would cost, never mind the effect it would have on the product's image and on mine?"

"Yours?"

"Yes, mine! I don't want to be remembered as the president who bankrupted the company."

"Well how can you tell the bad ones?" I asked.

"The longer heating period caused the coloration of the pills to turn a deeper color. They can be easily spotted or with a simple chemical test can be detected. My reputation is at stake here."

After he said this, it was obvious that his personal reputation was all he was worried about. The waiter started to come over but I motioned him away. I became aware of two men sitting at a far table who seemed to be having a hard time hearing our conversation. They were both physically built like weight lifters. Mr. Fields hit the table with his spoon. I don't know whether or not it was intentional but it was enough to gain my attention.

"I came here to hear your plan," he said.

"Here is your damn money," he said, pointing to the envelope on the table. "Let's hear it."

Before I could say a word, a young lady came into the dining room and by the way she walked into the table and chairs, it was obvious to me that she wanted her presence known. She was about six-feet-tall but with her heels she looked much taller. Fields mentioned for her to join us. Before I could say anything, he introduced her. "This is Miss Smith, it is not an alias, it is her name…she is acting as my assistant on the matter…I asked her here to help me evaluate your plan and to act as the go between… I can't keep coming to see you. It will create too much talk…everyone is wondering now why I am coming to this place…it will be better all the way around if she acts as our go-between…I think you can understand that. Also, she was the detective I hired to check you out before I hired you."

"I guess I passed her test?"

"Well, let's just say you didn't fail it."

He said the words as though they were rehearsed. Miss Smith had extended her hand out to me and I noticed that her nails were cut short. They didn't go with this tall, slender muscular lady. Her clothes were tailored and of the finest quality. Her hands were muscular with enlarged knuckles. They reminded me of a fighter's hands. As I shook her hand I could feel the strength in them. She smiled and sat down across the table from me. Mr. Fields, during this time, had picked up the envelope with the money in it and put it in his inside jacket pocket.

The waiter came back and Mr. Fields, who was visibly annoyed, turned to the waiter. "Give us three of this," he said as he opened the menu and pointed to one of the entrees. It was obvious that he didn't know what he ordered, but just wanted to get rid of the waiter. "We don't want anything else," he barked as the waiter took the menus back and left.

"Excuse me a moment," I said as I got up and walked into the men's room that was located between the bar and the dining room. The men's room had two doors, one that led to the dining area and the other to the bar. I walked into the men's room, making sure I wasn't followed, and walked into the bar. Before I had left my office, I had called a man I knew and asked him to meet me at the restaurant.

He was known as "The Head." His real name was Tony. He got the name because of the big round face he had and the curly blond hair that he wore like a mane on a lion. He was about six-feet-tall and very powerfully built. I had defended him two years earlier on a fighting charge. He had been in a bar and for some reason it never came out during the trial why three men had jumped him. He had put all three in the hospital but the reason he was being charged was that when the fourth man came over, he bit off the tip of his nose. The headlines read "He Ate My Nose." When I got a hung jury, the state didn't want another trial. I made him plea to a much lesser charge and he was freed. Tony was very thankful and besides paying me, he vowed his loyalty. I had called him because I felt uncomfortable about meeting Mr. Fields again. I looked into the bar, I saw Tony...he saw me and he waved...I went back into the bathroom and exited into the dining area. Mr. Fields looked up and half shouted, "Let's get on with it, I came here to hear your plan." The two men that were sitting in the back of the restaurant had moved so that they were now seated between me and the door marked "Exit." I could see one of them had something in his ear. I didn't know why but I felt he wanted me to see this thing in his ear.

"George, please," Mr. Fields said in a pleading voice. I sat down, took some notes out of my pocket and started.

"We have to divert attention from the company to someone else or something else. The normal flow of the goods would be from you, the manufacturer to the retailer to the user. To try to blame the stores would be impossible since we don't know where the pills are and even if we did, to get them all to agree would be an enormous task. Even if they all agreed, to try to settle with all of the users would cost a fortune and again I don't think it is achievable."

"Fine," Mr. Fields interjected. "I know what we can't do, what can we do?"

"Please." I said. "What we can do is create a monster." Field's face turned red. "Please be still," I said before he could say anything. We have to find one person who we can develop a cover story for...have him confess to purposely tampering with the product and, after he is indicted, defend him. By using doctors, we can give him a 'mental defense,' have him committed for a year or two to a mental institution, and when the heat goes away, get him out. The case will be handled down in Trenton and I think it's a do-able plan. The man selected will have to be well schooled in the procedure of how the poison got from the factory to the public, and the symptoms of the mental illness we want. I'm assuming your publicity department will write what I tell them."

Mr. Fields, without speaking, nodded his approval.

"The company will act shocked at what happened and immediately contact anyone who has the pills and assure the public all fifty of the pills have been retrieved. You will have to change the story on how the mistake happened to a story that the man made the pills and specifically inserted them into the distribution flow. Again, I'm assuming this can be done, namely, that someone could make their own pills." Again, Mr. Fields nodded.

"The people who you assign to work on this project need not know about the truth, only that if they don't keep quiet they will never work again." There was a deadly type of silence that settled over the room. Everyone and everything seemed to be frozen in space and time. I couldn't hear the din that usually came from the bar. After which seemed like an eternity, Mr. Fields nodded. Half struggling, he started to get up. His face looked pale even in the dimly lit room.

In a very hoarse voice he said, "I will have to get back to you. I have to think about this, I have to go." While he said this, he sat back down and nodded to Miss Smith and in the same low voice said, "Get him away from me."

While this was going on I had put my notes back into my pocket. Miss Smith stood up and motioned for me to stand. The two men that were seated at the table were now standing. I extended my hand out for Mr. Fields to pay me but he repeated again, "Get him out of here." His voice was still hoarse and barely audible.

Miss Smith lunged at me, but I pushed the table into her. The two men came at me at the same time the waiter was coming out of the kitchen carrying a tray with three pots steaming of the hot food we had ordered. Behind me the bathroom door slammed open and Tony came bounding out. In one motion he pushed me aside, knocked Miss Smith back with the table again, grabbed the tray from the waiter and threw it into the faces of the two men. One man put his hand out to block it and Tony bit his finger right down to the bone. Blood splattered all over. The big man fell to the floor with blood pouring from his finger. The other man, while trying to take the microphone from his ear, was at the same time trying to brush the hot liquid from his face, hands and clothing. Miss Smith started to vomit. She ran into the men's room. Mr. Fields stood up, turned ash white and fell to the floor in a heap. The waiter put his hands on top of his head and was shouting, "Help, Help me" while running in a circle. He kept banging into the table and chairs. Everyone from the bar came running into the room and after seeing the two men especially the one who was still bleeding started shouting. "Call a doctor, call the police!" Tony stepped back into the crowd and started yelling also. I reached down and motioned for one of the patrons to help me lay Mr. Fields flat on the floor. He was ash white and I didn't think he was breathing. The patron started pumping on his chest. He seemed like he knew what he was doing.

I took off Field's jacket, loosened his tie and the man was shouting orders to other people so I took the jacket and got out of the way. I took the envelope out of it, placed it in mine and folded the jacket over the chair. The doors to the dining room opened again and a police officer came in. The first policeman took one look and turned to run out the emergency exit door. A second officer came in and started moving everyone back. Soon the whole room became filled with police, ambulance workers, passers-by and everyone else who was in the area. Mr. Fields was given oxygen, put on a stretcher and taken out. The other two men were placed on stretchers and wheeled out the emergency exit. One had an enormous bandage around his hand. One of the attendants asked me if I were all right since I was covered with blood and gravy. I didn't answer. I buttoned my jacket after I made sure the envelope was still in it as I was helped out to one of the police cars and driven to the hospital. The doctor gave me a pill and just told me to rest easily. I was driven to police headquarters. The next thing I knew, I was sitting in a chair with two officers firing questions at me. I just got up and went to the bathroom to wash my face. I was trying to stall for time, so to somehow regain my composure. I refused to answer any questions. I inquired as to how Mr. Fields was but did not get a response. I got up, and one officer kept screaming for me to sit down.

The door opened. An officer came in with all kinds of decorations on him. With him was a well-groomed young man who was introduced as my attorney. Within a few moments I was allowed to leave. Outside, another officer drove me back to my car. When I returned home I took the envelope from my jacket, got undressed and threw my badly stained suit and shirt away.

It was now close to two o'clock in the morning. I put Mr. Fields and his problems out of my mind and dismissed the whole incident as just one of those things.

The Cardinal was putting on a good front or else he was truly interested. The wine and fruit were disappearing, but his attention was still very keen. "I can assume the poor man who collapsed was all right? The one who had his finger bitten, what happened to him? For an intelligent man why did you resort to violence? You don't seem like a violent person."

"Sir, I was afraid they were going to kill me. I am not violent. Tony is. He is very violent. Remember your followers are willing to be eaten by the lions I'm not." The Cardinal saw his comment upset me so he motioned with his hand for me to continue. He settled back in his chair and seemed to be enjoying what he was hearing. I was very animated when I spoke. I could not sit still as I told the story. I even acted out some of the events I was describing.

# Chapter Five

I never heard another thing about the incident, meeting or anything. Six months passed and I had all but forgotten about the meeting with Mr. Fields. I never saw anything about the matter in the newspapers, so for all intent and purpose, the matter was dropped. John and Lynn moved to California and hired an attorney out there to continue their case against the Fields'. I was out. I bought tickets to see the show Jane Eyre but could not attend so I had to give them away. For the life of me I don't understand why I even bought them.

At the end of July I was in my office when the doorbell rang. My office was on the first floor of a two family house. As you enter the front door, there is a vestibule with a door leading to the first floor where my office was and the other lead to the upstairs apartment. There were four connecting rooms to the flat in which the desks and file cabinets were placed.

It was around one o'clock and usually I wasn't there so I didn't bother to answer it. The bell rang again and was accompanied by a light tap on the window. I got up, went to the door, opened it and there stood Miss Smith. She was dressed in a fine tailored outfit looking taller than before with her gorilla hands. I went to shut the door in her face.

"Please don't," she said. "If you don't talk to me, I'll get fired!" The words came out in a sing-song manner that didn't fit the person saying them. "Let me come in," she continued. "I promise to behave."

Before anything else was said, she was inside, closed the outside door behind her, locked it, walked into the inside office, and waited for me to enter; she shut the door and sat down after motioning for me to sit down. It was as though I were at her office instead of her being in mine. I sat down. Before I had a chance to say anything, she chatted away as one would do when talking to an old friend whom they haven't seen for years.

"They want me with you again." She fit that sentence in even though it was completely out of context. "I know you're annoyed," she said as she reached into her Coach pocket book type briefcase that seemed to appear out of nowhere. She produced an envelope. "Here is expense money and a gift certificate for two suits and four shirts, your other ones must be ruined. We want you to know that we are sorry for what happened and would like you to forget about what has happened or at least allow me to make it up to you. We want you to come to Saratoga for the races. We understand you own a boat, which is in the Passaic River right here. You can come by boat and dock at the marina in Saratoga."

She promptly produced a navigational book that included the inter-costal waterway via the Erie Canal to Saratoga. "We will be expecting you on August fifth. We will have a car waiting for you at the marina. From here it should take you less than a day," she said while pointing toward the Passaic River. She got up and reversed the process she used to come in to let herself out. From start to finish she wasn't in my office five minutes and I hadn't said a word. She was gone. There was a limo waiting for her outside that she got in and drove away. Still stunned, I locked the office, and left to go home.

Half confused, but more curious, when I got home, I opened the envelope and there was money and a gift certificate for two suits and four shirts. I was tempted to forget the whole meeting but figured after counting the money everyone deserved a second chance.

On the morning of August 5th, I pulled out of the marina and headed toward Saratoga.

To get to Saratoga from Belleville, you first have to go south. The Passaic River winds its way through Kearny, Harrison and Newark. The shoreline is covered with garbage. It is easy to see where some clean up has been attempted, but the pilings left over from docks long ago closed is a constant reminder to stay in the center of the channel.

The river has a nine-foot difference between high and low tide, which constantly exposes all the sunken logs, rocks and other obstacles just waiting to destroy an unsuspecting propeller. There is a certain amount of industry along the river, and the most noteworthy is a scrap yard that has a machine that grinds up cars. The cars are smashed down, to about 18 inches high and put on a conveyor belt that leads to the grinder. The smashed cars go in one side, and come out the other in pieces no longer than six inches. The metal is separated from the non-metal pieces, and both items are put into separate piles by two other conveyor belts. You can't see the actual grinding process, but just to see cars going in one side, and little pieces of metal coming out the other is mind-boggling.

The Passaic River flows to Newark Bay. Where the river meets the bay, there are docks for large tankers to dock while their cargo is pumped into large tanks. The area is known as The Tank Farm. Pipes lead from the dock to the many tanks located on the shore well back from the river. The bay changes colors depending upon what spilled that day, or what waste was dumped in the Passaic River. More recently, many environmental groups have been trying to clean the river and bay, but somehow, there always seems to be a spill. The joke still remains that walking on water is no great feat here."

I paused a few moments but the Cardinal did not react at all to my attempt at humor.

I continued with my description of the bay. It is a few miles long and about a mile wide. The bridges that cross it are of no classical design; they just get the job done. The bay ends at Staten Island and the waters flow to the right and left. The waterway, although only six miles, is the busiest stretch of water around. It's called the Kill Van Kull. Just before you get

to the end of the bay, there is an area known as Port Newark.
There are enormous cranes there that are used to unload the
large container ships that constantly inhabit its piers. The ships
are hundreds of feet long and high. Their cargo carrying
capacity is increased by the fact that containers are piled high
on their decks, which make the ships look as if they will topple
over. The length, width and height seemed to increase, as I got
closer in my 27-foot center console boat. All the ships that go to
the port come through the Kill Van Kull. The channel through
the waterway doesn't seem wide at all, and especially if one or
more of the large cargo ships are coming through while being
assisted by two or three tugs. The tugs are necessary because of
the turn they have to make to come from the Atlantic Ocean into
the Kill Van Kull. The large ships have to make another turn
into Newark Bay, and finally to berth in Port Newark for the
loading and unloading process. These large cargo ships with
their cargo piled high on deck have to pass under the Bayonne
Bridge, of which one can only be in awe since the ships don't
look like they'll make it. Also, in the Kill Van Kull, are piers
where oil ships tie up to unload their cargo into the awaiting oil
tanks...again, the color of the water depends on who forgot to
do what on any given day.

The Kill Van Kull runs into New York Harbor or more
precisely, where the Atlantic Ocean, Hudson River, Kill Van
Kull and Harlem River all meet. Between the different currents,
and the ships coming and going, including the cruise ships,
ferries and sightseeing boats and the ever changing tide,
negotiating a 27-foot boat through the maze of markers
becomes quite a feat. On a rough day, it's all one can do to stay
out of everyone's way, but on a clear day, as today was, I could
enjoy the sights of the Verrazano Bridge south of me, and the
New York City skyline in front of me. Of course, the most
awesome sight is the Statue of Liberty. No matter how many
times I pass it, I can't help getting a lump in my throat and tears

in my eyes as I sing one refrain of God Bless America. I could just feel what my father must have felt as his ship pulled past the statue to dock at Ellis Island in the new country.

The tip of Manhattan divides the water...Harlem River, Hell's Gate and Long Island Sound to the right...Hudson River, Erie Canal and all points east and north to the left. Although I had seen the sights many times, every time is as though it is my first. On my right, I see New York City, with its majestic backdrop of the World Trade Center and Empire State Building. On my left, decaying warehouses and ferry terminals of yore, with a patch of revitalization here and there as New Jersey was trying to clean up its side of the river. Straight ahead of me was the George Washington Bridge. Its magnificence's dominates the northern view as seen from a 27-foot open boat. North is where Saratoga is, so ducking my head while I passed under the bridge and enjoying the fact that the tide was coming in which aided me as I headed north.

It was a beautiful day and I was trying to recall everything that had transpired. My ability to concentrate on the prior events was constantly being interrupted. The breeze seemed to pick up in intensity as I thought about my school days. No matter how I tried to think about something else, the breeze would increase in intensity as it swirled around me and I was back in my class. I truly had never forgotten this one girl, but after so many years to have her so fixed in my mind that I could not concentrate on anything else was unnerving. There I was in the Hudson River recalling the exact details of my classroom. I started to envision some of the students but one in particular stood out even though I could not remember anything about her, or her name.

The time passed so quickly that, without realizing it, I was up by the Catskills when I was brought back to reality by the unmistakable sound of my propeller hitting the rocks. I had gone out of the channel. Luckily I was by the marina so I could limp in. Two hundred and seventy five dollars and one hour later I was on my way again, but this time not thinking about anything but driving the boat. While waiting for the repairs to be made I had remembered some story I had read in school where mermaids would sing and the music was so sweet that the sailors of old would lose control of the ship and crash upon the rocks. I now knew how they felt.

Just north of Albany is the first lock of the Erie Canal System. The land starts to change in altitude so the locks are needed to raise and lower the boats to the new level.

Passing through the locks is a full time job, so there was no more daydreaming. By nightfall, I pulled into the marina near Saratoga. The man in the marina was indeed waiting for me and quickly tied up my boat. An elderly man came over from an old cab and picked up my bags and put them into the trunk. Throughout the process, no one said a word. Every time I tried to say something, I was greeted with a flurry of activity. My boat was very simple. I had bought it a few years earlier. It was 27-feet long...had one motor...one seat and one steering wheel. That was it. There was no cabin or any other accessory except for a radio and compass. Because of the simplicity, it was easier to care for. I got into the cab. It had been a long day. I just sat back as I was taken to a motel outside of Saratoga. The driver told me that he would pick me up at 8 a.m. and I would be having breakfast at the track. I showered, walked to a nearby restaurant, ate, returned and went to sleep.

While dozing off, or dreaming, I don't know which, I heard without hearing and felt without being touched, someone from my class calling me. It was as though I were still on the boat daydreaming. The thoughts I had on the boat didn't leave me as I thought they would, but rather lingered to now, revisiting me. She was there and yet not there. I dismissed it from my mind again and finally fell asleep.

In the morning, right on time, my driver was there to take me to the track.

Saratoga itself is beautiful, the area is beautiful and the track is truly a sight to behold. Miss Smith greeted me as the cab pulled to the entranceway. She brought me to Mr. Fields who was seated alone at a table. There were many people in the room so I felt at ease and figured if they were going to do anything it would have been done by now. Mr. Fields got up and motioned me to sit in the chair next to him. He waved off Miss Smith. He looked around and when he saw a waiter he waved the waiter over who quickly bought to the table coffee and buns. When the waiter left as Fields started to talk.

"I know what I did was stupid, but the fact that you're here shows me that you're a business man. Your plan has been started. We have located and retrieved 26 pills to date before too much damage has been done. We have selected the perfect candidate to claim responsibility. We have him primed and ready, he just wants to meet you. He feels that since his life is going to be in someone's hands, he wants to meet him. Or them. He wants to know who will be protecting him."

Fields rambled on for about 10 more minutes not really saying anything new but rather saying the same thing two and three times. By now the restaurant was full. The prediction was for a beautiful day and a fast track. Traditionally, people came early to watch the workouts and drink champagne with breakfast. I guess the theory being, after a few drinks you didn't care what your horse did. I excused myself and started to leave when Mr. Fields handed me a piece of paper with a number on it. It was the amount I would be paid for helping out. Mr. Fields, once regaining my attention, explained that for political reasons I couldn't be brought out in the open, but they wanted me to work behind the scenes.

"Is the man here?" I asked.

Fields nodded "Yes."

"Where?"

Again, Fields nodded, and motioned me toward a short, fat

tweedle-dee type man. He looked like a pear. He looked perfect for the task. Miss Smith took him by the hand, the same way you would lead a child around and brought him to me. I told him to wait. For some reason I had to go downstairs. I didn't know why, but there was someone calling me. I had to go. I was being called from someone downstairs. I pointed to the man and said, "In a minute, I will meet you by the doorway leading to the grounds." He nodded his approval and as he started toward the designated spot, Miss Smith, started too.

"You stay here," I said. "I can talk to what's his name..."

"Henry," she responded.

I continued, "To Henry, without you."

She was visibly upset. She started to walk away but stopped, spun around as if to say something, but before she could, "Look," I said. "You'd better learn to listen when I speak or you're not going to be able to move. They may think you're cute with your macho attitude, but...well just leave."

She glanced over to Mr. Fields, who by now was standing up, waving to her to return. The incident upset me but I figured that we better get this straight right away. I motioned for Henry to leave and he did.

I walked to the middle of the betting area, looking around, but really not looking for anything. I was trying to calm myself down. Miss Smith was really starting to get to me. Her arrogant attitude was starting to affect my thinking to the point where I was questioning my own motivation for doing things. I kept asking myself whether or not I was doing something because it had to be done, or was it just to spite that bitch...Miss Smith. To get my mind off her and the entire situation, I began to drift into another dimension.

Being visited by an image or drifting off while awake to someplace else in time happens to most people, I guess. To hear people speak about their own Shangri-La is an acceptable practice...I guess. When these things happen too often, the person to whom they are happening to is described as weird…I guess. Not me, I was strong, both mentally and physically, and I would never allow anything or anybody to penetrate the mental armor I placed around myself. If, for a moment, an affectionate thought entered my mind that was unrelated to my family, I would dismiss it immediately. Even this constant vigil, though mental, protected me from the ravages of infidelity or emotions. Any relationship was like the balls in a pool game. Never getting involved with anyone, get very close but the moment they touch, each goes scurrying off in a different direction unfazed by being with the others.

It is with this type of mental attitude that trying to explain what happened to me that day becomes more difficult. I entered a strange arena, both physically and mentally. I was milling about trying to make the ultimate choice of which horse to bet on, and making sure Miss Smith wasn't around. I became aware that I was standing next to a tall slender woman. She was a little shorter than I, with brown hair and wearing a big white hat, the kind with the floppy brim, with a flower in the middle. I could hear her voice, but not really able to distinguish what she was saying. It sounded like a tune being played by some sort of instrument. I stood there as though someone were holding me. The woman became aware of me, I really don't know how, but she turned abruptly and there we were facing each other, not more than a foot apart. My breathing stopped as I just stared at this woman. I studied her every feature but her piercing hazel eyes hypnotized me. I couldn't make up my mind as to who she was. I told myself that I didn't know her while at the same time convincing myself I did.

Her eyes were brownish with a fire inside that made me feel completely at ease while at the same time embarrassed. We just stood there. The crowds were milling around us, her friends were looking at us and calling to her, I think, but these voices just seemed to melt into the overall din of the crowd. The announcer was saying something about the horses, I guess, but we were both oblivious to our surroundings. Finally, one of her friends came over and grabbed her arm but she didn't move and I couldn't. Everything stopped around us. It was as though we were in a different dimension where reality doesn't exist. I was too afraid to find out what the alternative is...reality versus what...I couldn't bring myself to accept the fact that there may be something beyond reality. By now I wasn't breathing, I couldn't hear anything, and the only thing I could do was stand there while my heart beat uncontrollably.

Her friends became annoyed and tugged again at her arm...she became annoyed and pulled her arm away. She started to walk away, but after a few steps she stopped and took a step back .She turned and looked at me again. I hadn't moved and I still wasn't breathing, I don't think.

"Excuse me," she said. "Do we know each other?"

"Not unless your name is..." I stopped talking. I wanted to name a name, but I didn't know what name to say...I wanted to say something, but no matter how I tried nothing came out...I felt like I was on the other side of a sound proof glass looking at the tall slender woman with no name...I was sure I knew her while at the same time absolutely positively I didn't know her at all. I remember asking myself, "What are you doing?"

The word I heard was "No!" I think I said it, but to this day I'm not sure. She walked away and the last thing I saw was the white hat, with a floppy brim with a flower on, it moving away from me, on the head of a tall slender lady with brown hair and hazel eyes. The hat stuck in my mind. It was off-white with an off-white flower placed in the front part of the brim. The more I thought about it, the less I thought of the person wearing it. Again, I dismissed the entire incident, resolved that it wasn't she, whoever "she" was. I was convinced that daydreaming was an acceptable part of living, even if one doesn't know what he is daydreaming about.

The people near me at the races were looking at me and asked if I were all right. "You look like hell...What's the matter...You okay?" These questions were fired at me all at once and I just waved them off and went about the business of the day.

By the time I had recomposed myself, Henry was pacing back and forth by the door. We walked outside and he was so nervous he was stuttering as we walked. He finally was able to articulate some words that I could make out.

"They promised me you could get me out. They said I'd get some money, they said my mother would get money and be placed in a fancy home. They said it. They told me to trust you, that is why I wanted to meet you."

"Do you know anything about me? Has anyone spoken to you about me? What makes you think I can do anything they said? Why are you doing this?" As I was speaking I was still thinking about that damn hat and the lady under it. I, again, had to stop and compose myself, so that I could continue walking.

"What's the big deal?" he responded. "My mother is sick and has to go into a home—I can't afford that—even if I could, it isn't half as nice as the one where they're going to send her to. What's my life? Where am I going? Women don't flock to me. People avoid me. I have never, in all my life, received the attention I'm receiving now. Where else, or what else can I do to earn the kind of money they're going to pay me?"

"Henry, I still don't understand why you wanted to meet me," I said not fully understanding him or his reasoning. "Surely, there's more to your life than this?"

"Not really," he responded. "When I asked the other people whose idea this was, no one gave me a straight answer. I asked Miss Smith and she told me about you. "She hates you, you know.""

We walked back inside. I walked over to Mr. Fields while Miss Smith led Henry away. Before I said anything, Mr. Fields stood up and motioned for me to walk with him to his car.

He finally turned to me. "We have twenty-six. Three more are to be delivered to you tonight at the motel. Henry will turn himself in tomorrow. Here is the private number of the other attorney who is heading up the defense team. Please speak only with him. Stay away from everyone else. Here is more expense money and money for you...don't give us any receipts...after today you don't exist as far as I am concerned. The lawyer and Miss Smith will deal with you...good-bye." By this time we had reached his car. I opened the door for him and shoved him inside. The driver turned to say something and I pushed the button to close the window.

"You are the only one I deal with...You pay...You will get me copies of everything I want...That's the way we work...I'll talk to the attorneys by phone and will meet them face to face with you and Miss Smith, that's all."

I looked around inside the car. "This is really nice. It's the first one I could fit in."

I exited the car. Miss Smith was standing there. "You going too?" I asked as I motioned to open the door again.

She shook her head "no."

"Okay...here is my cab." As I got into the cab, I took notice of the white hat going by. I got out...this is ridiculous...I half ran after the lady... "Excuse me"...the lady turned around and I was stunned and mortified...there was no flower! "Oh, please excuse me," I said. "I'm very sorry...I thought you were someone else...please forgive me!" I got in the cab and returned to my motel. About midnight, the phone rang and there was a knock on the door. I answered the phone, but there was no one on it. There was a knock at the door. I got up to answer the door; but before opening it, I looked through the peephole in the door; I couldn't see anyone. I slowly opened the door. There was no one there, just an envelope. I opened it. In it was a smaller plastic envelope with three pills in it. I put them in my shirt pocket and went back to bed. The rest of the night was uneventful. The next day, I returned home down the same river through the same locks wondering if I would be distracted again.

I didn't go back to Belleville, but rather to my homeport in Bayville. I arrived very late, but because I was familiar with the waters, had no problems finding my way back.

I made a note to call the attorney and requested that copies be made of everything including any notes and they be delivered to Miss Smith or Mr. Fields for delivery to me, and that I speak to everyone. To be on the safe side, I decided to tape the conversation and note the time. Since it was a toll call, I knew the phone company would record it. The three pills I had received I left in the envelope, and placed it in the compartment on the boat for my next meeting with Miss Smith.

The Cardinal who had been silent so far asked, "The woman at the track, the one with the hat, did Betsy ever wear a hat?"

"No, not that I remember," I responded.

"Yet, you felt you knew this woman, the one with the hat? You must truly be troubled. You story is more like an adventure tale than a confession." He saw the word "confession" made me cringe, so he quickly added, "Continue, for the more of this experience you share the better you will be able to deal with it."

I was amazed that he was still listening and genuinely interested, or at least it seemed that way.

The next day I called the attorney to set up a conference call with everyone involved, and to request the documents in the case so that I could hear from everyone as to what their ideas were. He flatly said "No! I am running the show and there will be no interference with me or my staff."

The attorney was local to the court where we were appearing in, and he knew everyone there. I didn't really want to argue with him so I didn't respond.

I met with Fields in the New York office. For this meeting, I had made an elaborate chart/list of all the possible players and the anticipated events. I took out the list of people involved, but of course their names were missing but the list was:

Prosecuting attorney
Head investigator
Psychiatrist
Typist
Assistant attorney
Jury (12, possibly 14)
Judge
Clerk

Fields looked at the list but he didn't quite understand. "George, what's this for? How does this help the case? Do you really think we can influence the decisions that will be made? I've asked Mr. Wilson, the lead attorney for the defense to join us." At this point, I got up and started to pack away my papers. Fields pleaded, "George, stay please; Mr. Wilson, who is going to handle the trial, has got to know what is going on. That's not an unreasonable request. Please let him join us. Field's voice took a whole different tone to it. He started to sound belligerent or annoyed. "There's a lot riding on this case; please."

Fields, without waiting for an answer, pressed a button and in a few moments the door behind Fields opened and in walked Mr. Wilson. He was the picture of what a lawyer should look like, well groomed right down to his manicured nails. His suit looked like it was still on the hanger. He wore his Phi Beta Kappa pin on his watch chain that went from one vest pocket to the other. His hair was bleached so that there was some gray over his temples. When he walked into the room, he looked like a dancer at the Harvest Moon Ball. Fields motioned him to sit down, which he managed to do without creasing anything. He didn't sit; he more or less slid into the chair. He picked up the list I had prepared and paused, took a deep breath, leaned back then forward as though he were about to deliver the Sermon on the Mount. "Gentlemen, I want to be up front about this. I, nor will my firm, be involved in any attempts whether direct or indirect to sway the unbiased opinion of anyone on this list. The only reason I am here is at the request of Mr. Fields in his capacity as president of the company we represent. I want everyone to be absolutely clear on this. At the first mention of an illegal activity or a questionable activity, I will excuse myself and the meeting will continue without benefit of any input from me or from my firm." He sat back in the chair obviously waiting for either Fields or me to talk.

I went first: "Get this son-of-a-bitch out of here or..." Before I could finish, Fields was on his feet. His face was bright red. At first he couldn't even speak, he calmed himself down as best he could.

"You pompous ass, how much was your billings to me last year? You will sit there, you will listen, you will tell me what you think or your firm will never get another nickel of work from the company. I will take every case you are handling away from you and tell George here to stop whatever else he's doing and only work full time to destroy you personally. And if that doesn't work or takes too long, I will authorize his friend to deal with you! Now George, as you were saying." Fields sat down with a deliberate thump.

"Fill in as many names as possible and try to distract them by other means," I said. "Have jobs offered to them, get to the girlfriends or boyfriends, have a background check on every one of them and we can see where they are vulnerable." Fields looked at Wilson and both men nodded their approval.

The next day Henry turned himself in to the district attorney as planned. He was charged with endangerment and a whole host of other charges since there now had been four incidents reported from the pills: A death, two severe sicknesses and one minor illness. That left 17 pills unaccounted for.

At the arraignment of Henry, the company could not get

directly involved but made certain representation to the court that for humanitarian reasons they would help the victims without admitting to any guilt. From this meeting a new word was introduced into the English language, "Tamper proof."

The defense of insanity or diminished mental capacity was immediately entered. The defense turned over its expert reports and waited breathlessly for the state's. At the same time, the company started publishing a want ad for a psychologist to head up the internal psychological testing and human resources department. They made sure that all of the experts used by the state got one and, that the experts were contacted by an employment agency or headhunter. They were following my plan and from all indications, it was working. Fields had everyone report their progress to him as it happened. He would, on a weekly schedule, contact me with all the information for my review and moderating. Fields agreed that Miss Smith would sit in court with her handbag that had inside it a large recording machine. It picked up everything. In addition, the transcripts of the trial were done expeditiously which means it is recorded and transcribed in one day. Miss Smith delivered all of these transcripts to my office daily.

Everything was going smoothly until the new assistant prosecutor was brought on board. His name was Angelo Raimo. He was not a nice man to say the least. He objected to everything and obviously saw the case as being his vehicle to bigger and better things. He was not married, nor did he have a girlfriend. There were no known vices, in fact he was considered to be the biggest stiff in the department. He didn't drink or smoke. As far as everyone was concerned, he was unapproachable.

Mr. Fields, after hearing these reports, wanted to set up a meeting with me. Miss Smith was sent to get me and bring me to the Ramada Inn on Route 3. The reason for this was the Inn had suites that consisted of four rooms, side-by-side. The end rooms have beds in them but the two middle rooms have the connecting wall taken out and in its place was a huge dining table with 12 chairs around. You can get to the suite through the front lobby or if you didn't want to be seen you could come through a back door, get on the elevator and no one would even know you were there. It was through the rear door that I entered and went directly to the meeting. Mr. Fields was already there pacing back and forth. The pacing continued while I sat down.

Finally, Mr. Fields half yelled, "I don't like the prosecutor. He's unreal. We had the head hunters contact him about openings in our legal department and he turns out to be a self-righteous son-of-a-bitch." Miss Smith was shocked since Mr. Fields was always the perfect gentleman.

"George, you have to do something. This guy is not human. Henry is wavering. It seems he doesn't have any faith in our defense team...He wants you to run the defense...Don't worry, I told him no! George, these are the problems that I want you to help out...What do we do with this?" His voice trailed off.

"You know, Mr. Fields, you should inform me before we meet as to the subject matter. Meeting you, going home and having to meet again doesn't make much sense." Fields was so wrapped up in his thoughts that he didn't even hear me. There was a knock at the door, Miss Smith answered it...It was the waiter delivering coffee and juice.

"I thought it would be easier this way Mr. Fields," Miss Smith said. "They told me..."

Before she could say anything else, Mr. Fields started again, "George, something has to be done. This guy is young, he's smart and he has the 'guts' to beat us. If Henry buckles, we are all in trouble. Did I tell you that they are keeping Henry under twenty-four-hour security now? The cops they are using are coming right from the academy...Raimo is picking them."

I finally had a chance to speak as everyone sat down at the table. "Do you know anything about Raimo's family?"

"He has none," Miss Smith interrupted.

"What about in Italy? He had to come from somebody." Miss Smith went to her briefcase and pulled out a personnel folder. "He comes from Salerno, Italy. His grandparents raised him. His father was in the Navy stationed in Salerno, when he met his mother. He was born in the states and is an only child. His mother and father died in a car accident in the states. His grandparents got custody and raised him in Salerno. His father had no family, but his mother had a whole bunch of them in Salerno. He is devoted to them. He sends money, writes to them every week, and visits them every year."

When she finished, Mr. Fields wanted to know why he hadn't been told before. "No one thought it was important," she replied. She tried to continue to talk but Fields waived her off.

"George, go to Italy and see what you can do, I can't go through channels and you've just heard what they think is important and what isn't. You can leave tomorrow. I'll..."

Before he finished the statement, I just got up and turned to leave. "Send me a copy of that file and I'll make my own arrangements. I'll keep you informed."

As I got up, I looked down at a pad I was scribbling on. I had only written one name...Betsy. I reached down and quickly tore the page off and put it in my pocket. When I got to the door, I opened it slowly. I wanted to give Tony a chance to get out of sight. I had called him and asked him to follow me in case I needed him.

The next day, Miss Smith brought a copy of the folder to my office and put inside the colored over copy in which the impression had been made. When I had left, Miss Smith grabbed the pad and lightly colored over it with a pencil. I was not in, so she left the folder in my mailbox.

When I returned to the office, I opened the folder and became flushed when I saw what she had done, infatuated and yet confused because I didn't know why I had printed...Betsy.

The Cardinal put down his glass that he was sipping from and said, "Oh, you knew her name. You must have, for you wrote it down."

"No, I didn't. I didn't write her name. I was scribbling on a pad, that's all it was. I hand written down some letters that's all."

The Cardinal smiled as he replied, "You knew her name. You just didn't know you knew it. Please excuse my interruption and continue."

"I read the report on Angelo Raimo. He came from Salerno, as did the Marino family. They knew Raimo's family very well. The Marino family ran Salerno. They had ruled the area since World War II. There had been a bloody battle in the town to see who should have control. The senior Marino was now about 75-years-old and relied on his oldest son to manage things. I had gotten this information from Russ. Russ knew everything. Russ was the one who got John and Lynn's case for me. Russ was a con man. There wasn't a con that he hadn't worked. Russ was very pleasant and extremely good-looking. The joke used to be that even married men turned around when he walked into a room. He worked part-time as a bartender in a club in New York where "the mob" occasionally hung out. He was said to have known everyone. If you wanted anything, to know anything, or be introduced to someone, he was the man.

He sold information and an introduction to people like a store sells its wares. I had met him a few years earlier when he was the co-defendant in a church scam. He and an accomplice had set up a church. They recruited other "members" to bring people, or marks as they were called into the church. Russ and his associate would convince the new members that the road to hell was paved with gold, so the more gold they gave to Russ; the easier it was to go to heaven. A local priest had reported Russ to the police when a "little old lady" didn't have money to give the priest because she had given it to Russ. I defended

Russ and his associates, and got the charges dropped to a misdemeanor. They were fined 50 dollars each plus some community service. After the case they had a big party for me. Occasionally we would get together for lunch or dinner. Russ was always pleasant to be with and knew everything. When I had called Russ about my problem, Russ made a few calls and was able to find out who ran things.

"George," he had said, "When you land in Rome, call a friend of mine, Sabatini; he will introduce you to the Marino's. If you can, try to go to their house I hear it's something else. Also, as you drive to it, they claim that there's a body under every tree. They use them like fertilizer." This last comment had him laughing so hard that he could just about say good-bye. Russ was always Russ's best audience.

I called Alitalia for a ticket to Rome leaving the next day. I called Fields and told him of my plans. Fields wanted me to take Miss Smith with me but I refused. When I was ready to leave for the airport I wanted to make sure I wasn't being followed. I called Russ and asked him to meet me at the airport and make sure no one followed me.

When I got to the airport, there was Miss Smith standing like a statue and following my every move. She walked over to me. "Did you get my note? It's a bad habit of yours writing things down especially with your heavy hand!" She half smiled and tried to make herself laugh. I didn't crack a smile but started to walk toward the Alitalia area. Miss Smith and her companion fell in line behind me. From the corner of my eye, I could see Russ working his way across the terminal. When I got to the top of the escalator I got off and Russ stepped in-between Miss Smith, her escort and me.

"Why are you following him?" Russ yelled out. "Are you after his body?" Miss Smith went to push Russ aside and he hugged her. "Don't follow him, stay with me!" he yelled. "You can show me your black belts and all…Oh, I love it!" He had caused such confusion that everyone came over to see the refined Miss Smith wrestle with Russ. Russ kept yelling. "She has a belt...a black one...isn't it great?" The man with her pushed past everyone and Russ stepped in front of him "Didn't you get cooked enough?" He continued. "You got nine and a half, now you want to try for eight." The man stopped cold in his tracks. With all the confusion, I slipped through the door and got on the Lufthansa plane for Frankfurt while Miss Smith and her friend had to run to get on Alitalia for Rome. After I had booked my flight on Alitalia, I also booked a flight on Lufthansa just in case.

Once in Frankfurt, I got on a train for Salerno. The train leaves Frankfurt and goes through the Alps, through Rome to Naples. The trip is over night but sleeping on the train in the First Class car isn't bad at all. Whizzing through the Italian Alps and countryside is quite an experience. Once in Naples, I got a car and drove to Salerno, very watchful that I wasn't being followed. I checked into the Jolly Tar Hotel in Salerno and called Tony's room to make sure he was there. On the flight over, I had decided not to call Sabatini, but to see how far I could get on my own.

The next morning I made inquiry as to where the Marinos lived. From the expressions on everyone's face I guessed they knew, but at the mention of the name they didn't understand English and excused themselves. I hailed a cab and told the driver to take me to Marino's house...now. The driver started to say something but I just repeated the word, "Now!" The cab pulled away slowly at first and finally picked up speed.

The Marinos lived a little outside of town behind the Soccer Stadium on the side of a mountain. You can't see the house from the road you have to go down a long lane with trees on both sides. I couldn't help remembering what Russ had said about the trees and now that I was there I believed it. Before we were half way down the road, two men stepped in front of the taxi.

The cabby came to an abrupt halt and the men started to converse. Since my Italian was very limited, I didn't understand what they were saying, so I motioned to the driver to continue. The two men were shocked at the way I ignored them. A third man, who was much younger than the first two, came out of the woods and walked over to the car. "May I help you?" he asked in perfect English. "You're on a private road...this is the Marino estate, or as you would say in America, a tree farm."

"My name is George and I have come to see Mr. Marino. Please ask these gentlemen to get out of the way so that I can continue."

"You want to see my father?"

"Yes," I replied. "Please tell your father I would like to see him. If now is a bad time, just ask him when I should come back."

The young Marino walked over to a tree. From behind the tree he pulled out a phone and spoke to someone. He came back to the car. "Who sent you?" he asked.

"No one," I replied. "If he's too busy to see me now, we will leave. Please tell my driver to take me back to the Jolly Tar hotel."

The young Marino said, "Well, let me help you, what is it you want?" This time his question was more of a plea. I was waiting for him to say "please."

"No, just have your father, I guess, call me when he will see me." The young man spoke to the cabby again, walked over to the phone in the tree, came back and made a motion to the two men who were still standing in front of the car. They stepped aside and the car continued through the lane of trees. At the end of the road was a circular driveway. Dead center was two big doors that looked like they belonged on a church rather than a house. Off to the left was a beautiful vineyard behind what looked like a hut made out of grapevines. I was motioned towards the table and chairs under the grapevines.

A maid came from the house and greeted me. "Mr. Marino will be here shortly, refresh yourself."

I was surprised that by the time she said that out came four men, the young man and three others who looked like his brothers.

They all sat down and the eldest one started talking first. "Who are you and what do you want from us?" The question was asked in a stern voice, but without a harsh tone. "Do you think you can just come busting in here?" Before he could finish, the senior Marino came out of the house and joined the group. There was a quick scurry around the table for the senior to sit down before the others sat.

"Mr. George, did you try our wine? We make our own, you know. Did you have a nice trip over?" He kept up the stream of cordial statements inquiring about my plane, train, and car ride. It was as though he had come with me. "How can we help you?" He finally hesitated long enough so that I could answer. When I started to speak, he motioned for his eldest son to pour me a glass of wine. He responded, but I got the distinct feeling he would have much rather poured it on me.

"Sir," I was finally able to get out. "I really don't know what you can do. My problem is that there is a prosecutor in the states, Raimo, who is being very hard to deal with."

Before I could finish, he interrupted, "I know the whole family, and they live over by the bakery. Angelo used to play with my sons right here in this yard." As he said that, he nodded to one of the boys. "Angelo adopted his mother's maiden name. My good friend Sabatini called me and explained the problem to me. Let me think about what we should do. Tomorrow night we are having a dinner party, you please come?" He got up as he motioned for one of his sons to take me to my cab. I got up and shook hands with everyone. I turned to leave and I tripped as I was walking around the table. Instinctively, I put out my hand to regain my balance and when it touched the side of the enclosure I realized it wasn't made of grapevines but of cement. It was just decorated and painted to look like a grapevine. My surprise showed on my face.

Before I could speak, the eldest boy said, "Yeah, it's cement, they called them bunkers or pill boxes or something. It was built during the war."

I continued regaining my composure as I got in to the cab. The cabby let out a sigh of relief as we left the farm. When I returned to the hotel, there was a note from Russ. It said:

"I thought you might forget, so I called Sabatini and explained everything to him. I told him to call the Marinos for you."

The note was signed, "Love, Russ."

The Cardinal interrupted me by saying, "Mr. Marino is well known in Italy. He is the type of person who is seldom seen and only mentioned in whispers. Your friend Russ must exert a great influence over people. Sabatini is better known but he, too, moves in shadows."

I replied, "If this is so, how do you know about them?" The Cardinal didn't like the question. I continued.

# Chapter Six

When I returned to the hotel I felt very tired. I got undressed and lay down to take a nap. My clothes were half in the bag and half thrown around the room. All of a sudden there was banging on the door.

"Mr. George, Mr. George from America, excuse me please, we don't know how this happened, please excuse..." The manager unlocked the door, dead bolt and all, and was in the room. He ordered three or four maids to pick up all the clothes and suit cases.

"I'm so sorry, can you ever excuse us?" I was being helped out of bed, I was trying to put on my pants but I was being hurried along.

The manager kept repeating, "Excuse, excuse, Mr. George, excuse." I was led down the hallway and up one flight of steps to the next floor while I was still trying to get my pants on straight.

On the next floor were the private suites. The doors were thrown open into a large, bright, airy sitting room. On the table in the middle of the room was a large bouquet of flowers, on the side table was a tray of fruit and nuts with bottles of red and white wine on either side. There was another set of doors that led to a bedroom that had an enormous bed in it. The room was huge. All my clothes were quickly put away, the drapes were drawn, and the bed turned down so that the nap that was interrupted could be resumed.

The manager herded everyone out of the room still repeating, "Excuse, excuse." I looked around in disbelief. I poured some wine and with a piece of fruit I walked into the bedroom. I resolved that if they were going to kill me I would be dead already. I lie down on the bed and finally fell asleep.

About 4 a.m., the phone rang. I groped to find the phone, but it was on the other side of the enormous bed. I rolled over and grabbed it. As I picked it up, a pleasant voice came over the phone.

"Hi, I'm Maria. You're up? Good. You can't sleep away your time in sunny Italy. Get ready I'll be there in a half-hour. The stores are opening and we have some shopping to do. I'm making reservations for dinner at eight. That should give us enough time to get everything done. See you."

The phone went dead. I felt ridiculous staring into an empty phone. I was still disoriented, but I figured I'd better hurry. A quick shower and shave were in order. I started to get dressed only to find my suit to be missing along with my white shirts. My shoes were gone too. By now I was awake. I went into the sitting room and there were my clothes, all neatly pressed hanging on a valet, the kind bellmen use. I promptly took inventory, as I got dressed. Shoes were there shined. Even my socks were pressed. There was a knock at the door but this time whoever it was waited until I unlocked the door dead bolt and all and let them in.

She was elegant, not pretty, not vivacious, but elegant. She was about my age. She looked like someone you would see sipping fine champagne in an advertisement. There I was one shoe on, shirt out of my pants and still open to the waist.

"I'm assuming you are going to invite me in." Before I could say or do anything she walked in, put her purse down, went to the rack of clothes, picked up my tie, mumbled something, and put it back down. "We'll get one," she said.

By now, I had regained my composure. "You're the one who called." Before she could answer, I grabbed the tie and went back into the bedroom to make the necessary adjustments to my clothing. When I came back I was in a more orderly fashion, but I had forgotten my shoe. I sat down to put it on. "Who are you and where are we going?"

"My name is Marie, I was sent by Mrs. Marino to assist you to get ready for tomorrow night. Also, I will be your interpreter in case one is needed as well as your guide and escort. We can pick up a new tie at the store."

I finished dressing and then asked, "Before we go, would you mind answering a question for me?"

"If I can, of course I will."

"What happened after I left the other day? By time I got back here I felt like a king."

Mr. Marino called me outside. I had been working in the house. As soon as the cab pulled away, the four boys all started talking at once. "Why are we helping this guy? Who the hell is he? Why did you invite him to the party? What are we going to do for him? What's his problem?"

Finally, the eldest boy hit the table with his hand as he yelled, "I'll solve his god damn problem!"

The father sat there and shook his head in disbelief. "Look at all of you. Who is he? He is a person who can come in here and turn my four sons into a bunch of lunatics, that's who he is. And you..." He continued motioning to his eldest boy, "What are you going to do, plant another tree?" The other boys started to laugh, but when the father looked at them they shut up.

"Mr. George is what and who we say he is. He's from America; everybody in town knows he's here. He pays his respects to us first. Everybody in town will know that as soon as the cab driver starts talking. We make Mr. George into something; we are something since he came from America to see us. You plant him and we will have an enemy we don't even know. We have enough trees. Sabatini from Rome called me. They want us to make Angelo think that his family may be in danger so that he will be easier to deal with. Think of how we can do that!" With this, the father walked away. The boys looked at each other and set about the planning of what they would do. At that point I left.

When Maria was done talking I finished buttoning my shirt and followed her out of the room into the hallway. When we were in the hallway, she asked, "Aren't you going to lock it?"

"Why?" I asked. "It doesn't seem to stop anyone. How do you open and close the dead bolt from the outside?" She never responded as we waited for the elevator and went downstairs.

"You speak perfect English, how come?"

"I teach at the University, English literature, and Italian poetry." We walked outside and she waived for the cab.

"I would have come in a private car but it attracts too much attention." She motioned me toward the same cab and cabby I had used before.

"I'm sure my tie will do that," I said as we got in. Maria gave the cab driver instructions as to where to go.

"The party tomorrow night is formal. I knew you wouldn't want to be the only one without a tuxedo so we are going to the store where they can fit you for one. I can show you the area a little bit. Afterwards we shall have dinner at the restaurant at eight o'clock." She went through the whole speech without breathing. I didn't know whether the Marino's were trying to be nice or I was their prisoner.

"Are you going to tuck me in afterwards?" I asked.

"If you like," she responded without even looking at me.

The ride to the store took about an hour and she provided a running commentary on everything we passed. When we arrived at the store, the owner was waiting. I walked in and he and his staff had me measured in minutes. They showed me different styles, but I nodded toward my caretaker so she could make all the decisions. I didn't know what they were talking about anyway. We walked around the area until it was time to go to the restaurant. On the way to the restaurant I played tour guide pointing out all the points of interest and going into great detail as to the origins of the buildings and people who lived there. She just laughed. "Mr. George from America, I didn't

71

realize you were so knowledgeable about my area."

"I'm not, but only to a person who is," I replied. Maria laughed as she appreciated what I had said. Her constant jabbering about the countryside stopped.

The restaurant she took me to was in an old house that didn't look like any restaurant I was used to but rather someone's home. We sat on the veranda and were served a delicious dinner. I didn't know what some of the food was but it tasted good so I didn't ask. Each course had its own wine to compliment it.

After dinner, Maria and I went back to the hotel where I got out and shut the door before she could get out. "What time tomorrow night?" I asked through the window. She started to say something but I cut her off. "Tomorrow night," I said more emphatically.

"Seven thirty, I'll come and..." Maria started to say.

Before she finished, I said, "I'll meet you there." I went upstairs to sleep. No interruptions, except for Tony who called from his room in the hotel to wish me a good night.

The next morning was beautiful, so I just spent the day walking around town, having breakfast in the cafe in the center of town and talking to whomever I could understand. One man came over and during the conversation told me about an area about 20 miles south of Salerno which was very beautiful. He told me the name of a hotel to stay in on the beach. It was where the "locals" go. He wrote everything down for me and I put it in my wallet. On my return to the hotel, my clothes were delivered and the deliveryman insisted I try them on before he left. Everything fit perfectly. I told him I would leave them at the hotel when I left. He was shocked by the fact that I didn't want to keep them.

Before he could reply, I told him "thank-you," but I didn't want them. I'm not sure he understood me but he understood when I told him again I didn't want the damn clothes. He left shaking, his head muttering something. A nap, a shower and I was ready to go at 7 p.m. There was my cabby waiting by the door.

The drive to the Marino's seemed much shorter this time. As we pulled in the lane, we were in a line of cars going to the party. When it was our turn, a rather large gentleman opened the door and immediately the people opened an aisle. Everyone stared at me. I felt very uncomfortable as I walked into the room. Maria immediately greeted me. She really was stunning in her jet-black gown that seem to glisten with a light all its own. In her hair flowers were intertwined. She smiled at me as she quickly scanned my outfit and after she nodded her approval she brought me over and introduced me to Mr. and Mrs. Marino. As I looked around I could see everyone was in formal attire.

The room was beautifully decorated. There were about 50 people and everyone knew everyone else except me. I was introduced to everyone as Mr. George from America. Those were the only words I understood since everybody spoke Italian. Mrs. Marino was an absolute delight, as she would introduce me to someone make a comment, and laugh. Her laugh was very infectious so I found myself laughing when I didn't know why. Maria never left my side, constantly informing me whom I was meeting, what they were saying and why I should laugh.

Finally, we ran out of people to meet. I half dragged Maria to a window that looked like it led to a balcony. I grabbed two glasses of wine from one of the waiters and motioned her to open the doors. She laughed. I must admit I got rather annoyed. She reached over, took the glasses from me and motioned for me to open the door. I went to it and realized it wasn't a door to outside at all. There was no outside. It was just painted there. I stepped back or rather recoiled.

Maria came next to me as she said, "Close your mouth." I

didn't realize I was standing there gapping as I looked at the wall. "We're in a cave," she continued. The doors are only at the front. It was a bunker the Germans built during the war. It goes further back into the mountain. The light and scenery you see behind the windows are painted there with the lights being adjusted accordingly. No matter what else we did, or did not do, that night, nothing could take my mind off the fact that I was in a cave. The string trio that played all evening couldn't distract me for a moment.

At the end of the party, everyone I met coming in waited to wish me a "good night" on the way out. Maria, always by my side, kept a running commentary as they marched past.

When it was my turn to leave, the senior Mr. Marino came over with his four sons trailing behind, each wishing me well and the last person was the senior Mr. Marino. He kissed me good-bye and whispered in my ear, "Everything is done, you will be happy." I left the party, got in my cab for the ride to the hotel.

When I got to the hotel it was deserted. I hadn't realized how late it was. I got out of the cab, turned to pay the driver, or give him a tip, but he quickly pulled away. I went up to my room and got ready for bed. I looked on my dresser and there was a big brown envelope sitting there. It was the kind photographers use. In it was a picture of the entire Raimo family sitting with Mr. Marino with two of his boys on either end of the group. I hadn't seen the Raimo but in the envelope was a note explaining who they were, "The whole Raimo family surrounded by the Marinos." I put the picture away and went to sleep.

In the morning I called Tony and told him to go home, for I wouldn't need him. I checked out and got into a car I had rented. I just felt tired. I didn't want to go home. I remembered the note in my wallet so I went back inside to the clerk and asked him how to get to the place written thereon. He came outside with me and pointed to the road I should take. "Straight, straight," he kept saying. I went for a ride around town past the Marino house and finally asked directions back to the hotel so I could start my journey to the hotel on the beach.

I drove for a while when I saw a little sign bearing the name of the hotel with an arrow. I followed it around the curves that led me to the beach area which brought me to the front of the hotel. It was just as described, right on the beach. I requested and was brought to a large airy room overlooking the Mediterranean. There were doors that led out onto a walkway that led to the beach. There were tables and chairs set up under a big grapevine. This was a real grapevine. A waiter was standing there waiting to be summoned. Beyond the table and chairs area was a sandy, gritty, gray beach that led to the sea. All in all, it was just as described to me by the clerk in Salerno. I changed into my swimsuit and sat by the beach for the rest of the day reading an English newspaper. During the day I called my office and was informed that five more pills were found. That night after dinner, I decided to take a walk on the beach. I changed out of my suit I had worn for dinner and into a more casual outfit complete with sandals.

As I walked down to the beach from the hotel I looked out into the blackness that shrouded the Mediterranean. I could hear the waves beating a rhythmic tune on the shore. The sound was my guide, for nothing else could be seen. The combination of the melodious tune and the absent of light had a sort of hypnotic effect on me as each part of my consciousness began to shut down. The gentle breeze that was blowing accented the solitude I felt as it swirled about me as it searched for a place to settle. I saw something coming towards the beach but I could not recognize what it was. The thing started to take the shape of a human the closer it got. Suddenly, it was in front of me. I had to blink to bring my eyes in focus, for I feared what I saw. For a split moment I lost consciousness. I was again alert.

She was there.

Betsy.

When I went back to my room I saw her there as well. In the morning I drove to the Vatican. I went to St. Peters and that is where I met the old man. He brought me to you.

The Cardinal and I had started to move around the garden again. We stopped walking and went back to sitting on one of the ornate benches in the garden. I hadn't taken notice of the table that had been set up next to us with little sandwiches and a bottle of wine and water. The Cardinal got up, blessed the food, and motioned for me to help myself as he poured two glasses of wine.

I didn't realize how long I was with the Cardinal or how hungry I was until I tried to get up off the bench. I asked where the men's room was, and by time I got back, there had been two chairs added to the table as well as more food. There now was a complete array of Italian foods being offered as well as red and white wine. The Cardinal could sense my uneasiness. He motioned for me to sit down in the other chair and as soon as I was comfortable, started the conversation with, "Two others were to be here to have lunch with us today but I have been informed they will not be able to make it. One of the things I miss most by being a Cardinal is the daily contact I used to have with people. This is really a treat for me to have lunch with a parishioner."

"Your Eminence, I think you're just saying that so I don't feel so guilty for taking up so much of your time." As I spoke I felt as though a great weight had been lifted off me.

"Calling a Cardinal a liar? Really, George, I mean it. I take this time with you so that someday you will also make the time to help another person understand something that is troubling them. I have listened and I don't profess to know the answer to this pill problem. I am going to assume you will continue to try to get the bad ones back. As far as the Betsy problem, find her.

Why don't you just find her? You have the knowledge and friends to do that. Maybe she is calling you or maybe it is something you always wanted to do but you became so engrossed in your own life that you buried her deep in your heart. When you did that it created a scar. For, contrary to what the doctors say, the heart never heals. The physical side might but not the emotional side. That scar will always be present. Find her and that should go a long way towards helping you find some peace of mind. It will never heal the wound but it may help you find a better way of dealing with it. But now I must go."

"Father, I mean your Eminence."

"No, 'Father' is just fine. I love being a priest. My order decided that I could better serve God as a Cardinal."

"I would like to do something for the old man. Please tell me how?'"

"Old man," he added. "My novice will take care of that for you. Just tell him what you want done and he will do it." As the Cardinal spoke the young novice reappeared out of nowhere. The Cardinal got up, shook my hand, turned and disappeared into one of the doorways.

His abrupt exit left me startled for a minute as the novice said, "This way sir."

As I was led back to the guard station I came in I explained that I wanted to give money to the old man and I wanted to make a contribution to the cardinal and to pay for the lunch. He handed me a piece of paper with his name address and phone number on it.

"Send me what you want, along with instructions as to what I am to do, and I shall see that it gets done. Excuse me, but I have to leave."

With those words, the novice disappeared and I went back to my hotel, resolved to return to the states and solve my problems. I felt better, but I didn't know why. That Cardinal didn't help me. Or did he? That night I said my prayers. Something I hadn't done in a long, long time. I was resolved that the next day I was going home.

I had to go home immediately. I couldn't understand why what happened, happened, but I knew I had to get back to familiar surroundings. I felt out of place being in a foreign country. I realized that I was born and lived my life up to that point within a very small radius. To have an experience like I just had would be bad enough, but to have it in a foreign place just added intensity to it. To not be able to explain it was the worst part of all.

I changed my ticket after a great deal of arguing, but finally convinced the authorities that the plane was not leaving without me. I returned the car at the airport, in Rome, and waited for the next plane that would take me home.

Upon my arrival home I read the note the novice had given me and sent him a check to be divided up as he saw fit. I was now determined to find out where Betsy was, but again, my traditional upbringing stopped me. Unfortunately, it did not stop the thought of this woman from haunting my very being.

# Chapter Seven

When I came back to the states, Miss Smith greeted me. She started rambling. "I had to constantly keep in touch with our friends in Italy to see when you left so that I could be here to greet you. You must think that I'm..."

Before she could finish I handed her my small bag to carry. We walked out of the terminal where she had a car waiting for us. The driver opened the trunk for the luggage and once the bags were loaded we were on our way.

In the car Miss Smith started again. "You are very lucky that Mr. Fields doesn't turn me loose on you. But if I were you, I wouldn't count on his good nature." By now she had seen that I had gone to sleep. She reached over and shook me.

"What is your problem?" I asked. "If you don't like the arrangements, quit, but don't bother me again or you're going to see a side of me you don't want."

"Is that a threat?"

"Yes, now leave me alone." After making my speech, I went back to sleep.

We arrived at Mr. Field's apartment in New York City. Miss Smith woke me. The doorman opened my door and we went in. Mr. Fields was there with the trial attorney, Mr. Wilson. The attorney immediately excused himself and left. Fields turned to me. "That picture was pure genius. Someone sent me a copy. The trial starts in two days. That picture was placed on Raimo's pillow last night. It may not be a horse head but it will have to do." He chuckled to himself, handed me an envelope and went into the other room. Miss Smith just stood there obviously annoyed by being shunned. I looked at her, turned and left. The driver who was waiting for me took me home to familiar surroundings and my own bed which were a welcome sight.

Just being home was enough for me to enjoy a great joy. I felt safe and secure in my own home.

Raimo woke up and after he saw the picture, called his grandparents. Mr. Fields had taken the precaution of having Raimo's phone taped so the whole conversation was made available to me almost as fast as he hung up. His grandparent's hearing was very bad so he tried to explain his concerns to one of the children. About half way through it he stopped since what he was concerned about sounded ridiculous to him. "How come you took this picture with the Marinos?" he kept shouting into the phone. "How come?" he yelled again. There was a discussion held on the other end of the phone but he couldn't make it out. Finally someone came back on the phone.

"Mr. Marino invited us over for a picnic, you know, like we used to do when you were here...After a while this man come out with a big camera and took our picture...Everybody together...He gave us all one...Mr. Marino said we're all one big happy family...You know, like before you become a prosecutor or whatever it is you do over there...Mr. Marino says it's sad you're not here practicing law, you should be with us like before but he will send a picture to you with his wife's friend, you know, Maria. You remember Maria. She met Mr. George from America and Mr. Marino was sending you the picture and asked Maria to ask Mr. George to bring it to you when he got home."

The person on the phone kept talking, telling him about the big party that was held at the Marino's that night...they weren't invited but Mr. George was. Raimo was stunned by what he heard. Finally, they hung up. Raimo walked around his room in a kind of stupor before deciding to call George. He was hesitant about contacting George, but resolved he had to. He picked up the phone and called. He had gotten George's number from information. "Hello, Mr. George from America, is that you?" he asked. "I would like to meet with you as soon as possible. I don't know if you know me or not, but your name came up in conversation in regard to a case I'm working on and I really need to talk to you, so could you possibly alter your schedule so that we could meet as soon..."

"We'll meet," I interrupted. "I heard of you but you sound like you're...well never mind. Where and when?"

Raimo thought awhile and suggested Olga's Diner where Route 70 and 73 meet outside of Camden. A mutual time was selected and the matter was put to rest. Russ, who had been sitting with me when the call came in, had gone to another phone to listen in. "George," he started. "You know it's a set-up. They're going to wire him like a radio. They're going to try to get you to say anything that will allow them to indict you for some kind of tampering."

I looked at Russ. "I know, but what can I do. If I don't go, they'll think I'm afraid and I'll never get rid of them. If I go, dear Mr. Raimo will learn that we're not afraid and we have long arms if need be. In any event, I'm going."

At the appointed hour, I arrived at the diner and had Tony with me. "If they make a move on me, stop them."

Tony entered first and sat at the counter with the rest of the crowd but positioned himself so that he could see the whole diner. I waited a few minutes and walked in. I stood in the entranceway for some time and when no one acknowledged me, I turned to leave.

Mr. Raimo sprang to his feet and started yelling, "Mr. George from America." I stopped and turned around to meet Mr. Raimo.

"I forget to ask what you looked like," I said. "How did you know me? Oh, never mind. Where are we seated?" I followed Raimo to the table and quickly ordered something.

As soon as the waitress left I looked at him and could see he was very nervous. I waited for a few moments before I said, "Now what can I do for you, Mr. Raimo? You seemed quite anxious over the phone."

Raimo looked at me for a long moment before he blurted out, "I am trying a case and I think someone is trying to pressure me into losing," he said. The words came out like a sword being thrust in a dueling match. "I want it understood that that's not going to happen." His tone, now, was very authoritative. "I'm going to try this case..."

I interrupted. "What case and how am I connected with it? And please, sir, stop the theatrics or threats or whatever it is you're doing. I came here to give you a gift from Mr. Marino and out of curiosity since I don't know you and I still don't know why I'm here...It seems as though you're having a nervous breakdown and maybe you should calm down before you tell me what you're talking about."

Raimo shouted, "I'm talking about you threatening me by giving me this picture with my family surrounded by the Marino's! I had the airlines check to see who came into the country and by the process of elimination I came upon your name! I was going to have an investigator call you but after thinking about it some more decided to call you myself! So I know you were in Italy and I heard about the reception party they had for you!"

"Mr. Raimo, I didn't give you any photo. The photo I have is here in this envelope. I don't know where you got that picture. It certainly didn't come from me."

Raimo looked and saw that I had in fact placed an envelope next to him on the table. "Don't think for a moment that I'm going to..." he started to say.

I interrupted. "Please don't make veiled threats. I am not impressed. You wanted to see me I'm here. If you want to ask me something, go ahead and ask but stop with these accusations. I think you're having a nervous breakdown. I don't know why they would allow you to handle any case. As far as the Marino's go, they seemed to me to be nice people but I really don't know them."

"They had a party for you, or at least you were invited..." Raimo continued.

I looked at him. "I wasn't invited. I met a lady, Maria, and she was invited. I was her escort, that's all. You really are having a breakdown...you should practice law in a more sedate atmosphere...like in Salerno. If there isn't anything else, here is your picture and I'm going and I would appreciate it if you would stop checking up on me. It's illegal to say the least."

Raimo got up but this time without the arrogance he had shown since I met him. No threats. In fact, from the proud young man he turned into a humble, pleading person. When we got to the door he grabbed my arm. "What should I do, what should I do?" he pleaded.

"You should have a breakdown and go back to Salerno," I whispered in his ear as I left.

I drove home to start to prepare for the upcoming trial. There were many more meetings and more preparations, until finally; the day arrived...the first day of court.

The courtroom was packed. Angelo had been denied a postponement and his boss refused to take him off the case. Angelo felt the picture was a warning that he had better not try too hard. One day in the courthouse he got into a shouting match with his boss. The argument seemed staged to the onlookers because it was out of character that his boss would behave as badly as he did.

His boss, in a loud clear voice, warned him, "For a picture...we'll investigate but who...your family...the defense...Where do we start?...No Angelo, you insisted on this trial...The man confessed...The company is helping the victim...The experts say the defendant is nuts...We could have just taken the plea, the judge would put him away and that would have been the end of it...You now have this office involved in a trial where our own experts are wishy-washy…Just so you can be a hero. You insisted on a first-degree murder charge. You said you were going to convince twelve people that he's not nuts so the state could kill him. Now do it!"

The feeling was that Angelo's boss wanted everyone to know that trying the case wasn't his idea. Also the rumor was that his boss wanted me to know that he knew what I had done. I believed the rumors because that is usually the kind of conversation one would have behind closed doors not in the lobby of the courthouse.

The jury selection took weeks since the trial wasn't only about innocence or guilt but rather was he sane or insane. The question had not been dealt with in quite that fashion. The judge had entered an innocent plea and wanted the trial to proceed along those lines like any other trial. The defense objected, since to enter an innocent plea would require the state to prove each and every element of the trial. The jury would be bombarded with testimony that would prove the guilt and which might influence them that Henry was not insane rather than basing that decision on the expert's testimony alone.

Mr. Raimo in his arguments stated that the whole truth must be shown to the court to allow the jury to decide whether or not they believed the expert. "After all, your honor, an expert's opinion is like any other piece of evidence. It can be accepted or rejected by the jury…it doesn't have to be believed by them."

The defense position was that the jury may well be swayed by the expert's testimony on the theory that insane or not, let's get him. Between my presence in the courtroom and the tape recorder in Miss Smith's pocketbook I was kept up to date as to everything that was happening. There was no attempt made to shield the facts that I was involved.

At one point the judge asked, "Will the real defense attorney please approach the bench?"

Mr. Wilson became infuriated but quickly responded, "I am the real attorney for the defense."

The judge had at first reserved his decision about having the trial but was pressured by his bosses to resolve it quickly. By now, other foreign objects were being found in other products. Every manufacturer was producing tamper proof containers. The increase in cost, like all additional costs, was being passed on to the consumers.

The judge came back to the bench the next morning. "I have heard arguments from both sides and I have resolved to rule in favor of the State. A full trial will be held, an innocent plea will be entered on behalf of the defendant, Henry. I will not accept any other motions in this matter that in any way delay this trial. Opening statements, tomorrow morning." All rose and the judge left.

When Fields heard the decision he was infuriated. "We are going to drag this thing out!" He shouted into the phone as he spoke to the lawyers. "Just plead him guilty."

The lead attorney, Jonathan Wilson, responded, "Sir, the state will not accept a guilty plea from a person who we have just said doesn't know the difference between right and wrong. The motion to have the trial decided without a jury would be extremely dangerous to attempt even though your Mr. George feels it is the way to go, you hired our firm because you felt that..."

Before he could finish, Fields interrupted. "I didn't hire your firm, the board of directors did, but I sure as hell will fire you if you don't start following instructions. Get rid of the jury, let one man make this decision not twelve...we don't know what they will do." Fields hung up the phone.

He turned to me and in an unusual stern voice asked, "Do you think you could have done better?" I did not answer but rather just left our daily meeting. Today's meeting was held in the company's apartment that was across the street from the court.

The motion to hear the case without a jury was denied. The

judge called for opening statements.

Raimo's opening statement traced the entire history of the crime. He made constant reference to the confession not per se, just quoted from it as to how the pills were switched. He said there was a confession but did not mention the fact that he was quoting from it when he was speaking. He did not comment on the mental capacity of the defendant at all other than: "You will hear testimony from experts as to the mental capacity of the defendant. You will have to make up your own minds as to the weight given to it." That was all. The judge felt uneasy as to the opening but didn't say anything. The defense waived their right to an opening statement.

"The less said in that court room, the better off we are. Don't cross examine, just prove our case for insanity or craziness or whatever else they call it." Field's words came over the phone loud and clear.

When he was done he looked at me. "Well?"

I kept quiet, as it seemed to me that Fields was losing his grip on things and I didn't really know what to do.

The trial progressed very quickly since Mr. Raimo was allowed to do anything he wanted as long as it didn't touch upon the mental capacity of Henry. Every day Henry was brought into a room for "special" grooming by the defense. At one point Raimo lost his composure and shouted, "Your honor, the defense is purposely making him look like an idiot! Look how he is dressed...The suit is too small...The shirt just about buttoning...His hair is combed like I don't know what!"

The judge became enraged. He had difficulty in controlling himself as he quietly asked the bailiff to remove the jury. After they had gone, he turned to Raimo but before he could say anything, Raimo tore into him. "I don't intend to stand here and have you berate me. If you want to rule, you rule but don't you shoot your mouth off to me!" At this, Raimo lunged for the judge. The bailiff came running over to subdue Raimo and he was shackled and carried from the court.

The judge sat at the bench visibly shaken for a long time before looking at Mr. Wilson. Finally he asked, "Does the defense have any motions?"

"No, your honor," was his response. He turned to see where I was and when our eyes met I nodded my agreement. The Judge saw it too.

"I will see council in my chambers!" he yelled.

Mr. Wilson sprang to his feet. "Your honor, I do not wish to be in your chambers without the state being present. This is a highly sensitive case and in all fairness to our client, I do not want even a hint of impropriety. Please have the state send a representative before I come to your chambers."

After what seemed an eternity the judge spoke in an almost inaudible tone. "Off the record." Mr. Wilson again jumped to his feet.

"Your honor, please, if you are going off the record, I am leaving. This isn't your own private domain. Anything that is said in connection with this case is on the record, or you can talk to yourself. I say this with all due respect, but the rules that govern me, govern you. Insane or not, the defendant still has his rights."

The judge was at a loss for words. "Court is dismissed until tomorrow morning at eleven o'clock," he said as he left the bench. "Dismiss the jury."

The judge called out to one of the assistants of the prosecutor and told him to review the record and to be in court tomorrow at 11 a.m. with his recommendations. He called Mr. Wilson's office and had his clerk relay the same message to him. Mr. Fields and I were in the office when the call came and we were both elated. That picture worked.

The trial was over in three days. The plea was accepted, the defendant, Henry was turned over to the mental institution for evaluation, and Henry was on his way to being a free man.

Although according to him, in jail he was being treated better than he ever was at home. His every wish was acted upon all under the guise of rehabilitation.

Six more pills were accounted for. One death and five people who were very sick.

Within a week, the sensationalism was taken out of the case; the final result was pushed to the middle of the newspaper, and finally dropped within a week.

Mr. Fields called for another meeting at the Ramada Inn. I came, but no Miss Smith. I was astonished. I entered the room. There was only Fields and myself present.

"George" he said. "Some of these pills are said to be in the Las Vegas area. Please go there and see the distributors, here are their names. One of them has the pills but wants something. Talk to him and let's end this thing." He sat down relieved that the end was now in sight.

"Where's your Miss Smith? I thought this would be the type of thing you would want her to do."

"Let's just leave Miss Smith out of this. You go and end this thing...please." The please almost knocked me over.

"Mr. Fields, you have been more than generous to me but I must tell you that I am having a bad problem with my blood pressure and my sugar. The damn pills they prescribed have affected my ability to function. I am constantly thirsty and constantly in the bathroom."

He started to smile but he saw that I was very somber when I said, "I don't know if I can do this for you. I am experiencing something that I don't understand and it starting to affect my..."

Before I could finish, Fields interrupted, "George, I want this over with and I think that these people in Las Vegas are just a bunch of crooks. My problem is I don't know right now whom else I can trust. I'll put this matter on hold for a month or two. Let them stew out there. Go take care of yourself and call me next month and we'll meet. Just tie up what loose ends there are and we will wait on the Las Vegas matter." Fields turned and left.

I could not believe what I had just heard. The coldest fish I had ever met sounded like a human being. I shrugged my shoulders and left.

In the month that followed, my plan began to come to an end as far as the court case was concerned. I was constantly on the psychiatrists to get Raimo examined. Raimo was kept for observation and within a week released. He returned to Salerno within a week to a hero's welcome and immediately was granted a license to practice law with a law office in Salerno. Maria saw to the details herself.

The judge, not quite understanding what happened; made a public statement that he would be leaving the bench because of personal and financial pressures. "My family must come first and with three children I can make more money in the private sector than I can ever make as a judge." He resigned and was immediately hired by Mr. Wilson's firm.

The first time he came face to face with me before I could say anything he greeted me with: "You played me like I was a piano." I didn't say a word. The fact I kept silent infuriated him.

Henry died. No one knows why, no one knows how, no one knows what happened to the body. The only thing left was a notation in the night nurse's log, "Patient succumbed at one o'clock...morgue called." The nurse who signed the sheet was fictional. The nurse who was on that night had seen nothing, heard nothing and knew nothing. The entire hospital staff all gave the same answers.

Two detectives were assigned to the case. One just shook his head in disbelief. "I'm going to get to the bottom..."

Before he could finish, the other detective inserted, "Be careful you don't stay on the bottom. As for me, I will file these reports and solve another missing person case since we really don't know if in fact a murder took place and if whoever did this, can leave a whole hospital deaf, dumb and blind. I don't think I really want to get too much involved."

The first detective was enraged and got up from his seat. The supervisor was walking through the office. "Sir!" he called out. "I want another partner assigned to me on this missing body case at the hospital."

The supervisor, without breaking stride, turned and asked, "What body?"

The detectives picked up the next missing person file.

# Chapter Eight

While I was watching TV, I received a call. The caller, whom I didn't recognize, stated that there was to be a meeting at the restaurant at 8 p.m. "Be there!"

I heard the message but had no reaction to it and continued watching the show. The phone rang again, but this time it was a voice I did recognize. It was Fields.

"George," he said, "Tomorrow; all right! We need to meet. Please come; you're the only one I can trust. Come, eight o'clock."

Before I could respond, the phone went dead.

I sat in my chair, completely oblivious to the TV blaring away. I asked myself, why me? I'm trying to get away from the business for a month or two. In that time I can beat this diabetes, constant thirst, and constant going to the bathroom. My temperament was too abrupt for what I felt had to be done.

I had gone to the friendly doctor who had an understanding of the profession I was in, but could not come up with an effective treatment that would lessen the effects of this illness, which was believed to be diabetes.

I called Mr. Fields and explained to him why I couldn't come. Between being haunted by a memory and affected by an illness I wasn't sure what to do. Fields started talking and he sounded really concerned. "George, I have dealt with the best of everything. Everyone goes through these peaks and valleys. It's these valleys that created God since we reach for help; and the peaks that created the devil since we don't need anyone and we are masters of our own faith."

By now I was staring at the phone not believing the words I was hearing or that they were coming from the person that they were. The last thing I felt like hearing was some sort of philosophical bullshit. "We'll meet," I half yelled into the phone. I wanted to shut him up.

The call that Fields wanted to have dinner brought the past events quickly back into focus. The restaurant and time were already picked. I just had to be ready. They were sending the car for me. All through dinner, I was constantly excusing myself to go to the bathroom and after a while the suggestion was made that we move the meeting into the men's room. It was after dinner that Fields had told me he had made an appointment for me the very next day to go to a certain clinic. Nothing was accomplished at the meeting except I was told that the group was pleased with the progress of things and decided that Las Vegas be put on hold until I could go.

The next day I went to the clinic that specialized in treating diabetes.

As I sat in the general waiting room I wanted to leave but at the same time knew I should stay, not for any reason except I felt horrible. Having to drink, while at the same time, having to go to the bathroom was just wearing me down. The deterioration process was both a mental and physical one. Physically, I always felt drained of any strength to do anything. Mentally, to quote a phrase, I was a basket case. I found that I could not think a problem all the way through nor did I feel comfortable with the decision making process that goes along with trying to figure out something. I was being put under a tremendous amount of pressure to continue the assignment since I had been "with it" from the very beginning. To eliminate the last of the pills and make it look as a natural thing was a tall order and the powers to be were very tense about having a new guy do it. The words they used kept going over and over like a bell. "You can do it, you're the only one, it'll be easy, this is the last part, we promise."

While I was sitting in the waiting room, there was a lot of activity with deliverymen, patients, doctors, nurses, and phones ringing. Through this din came a voice, "Will you please come with me?" Half conscious, I was led down a hall that had many doors to a little room in the back. I assumed all the other doors led to other examining rooms. The room was small and what little space there was filled with an examining table, a scale, a sink, two chairs, and a stool.

I followed the instructions that were being barked at me by the receptionist who led me to the room and in some vague way answered in a voice so low that the girl trying to record the information had to keep telling me to repeat myself. After what seemed to be an eternity, she finally shut up and left. Halfway out the door she turned and in a clear loud voice said, "Be seated, the doctor will be right with you." It was more like a command from a drill instructor, than a request to a patient. I couldn't sit but found myself walking around this little room. I took off my jacket and put it over one of the chairs. Finally, I sat on the examining table as the door opened.

Standing in the doorway was this little girl with eyes that sparkled. Her eyes just lit up the whole room. I found my eyes fixed on hers and as I now think back I cannot remember what she looked like or what she was wearing for that first meeting. She was small in frame, as she stood outlined by the doorway.

I was stunned, I don't know what I expected but this was ridiculous. I got up to leave but she started to talk and her words had a soothing effect, something like a cat's meow. I could not understand what she was saying but it was still pleasant to the ear. I sat back down and started to reexamine my motivation for being there. I wanted help, but I still wasn't sure why since to be healthy again meant I would have to continue the case, something I didn't want to do.

By now, she had traversed the room and had shut the door behind her. She said something and I just laughed. The more I wanted to stop, the worse it was. She got such a hurt look on her face which went right through me.

I stopped laughing while she bombarded me with more questions. Her calm singsong voice and mannerisms were completely disarming so that I felt completely at ease. She kept jabbering away and I would nod or react in some way to answer her questions. The light scent of her perfume acted to further sedate me into some kind of trance.

"What did you use to do, or what do you do now?" she asked. The questions just flowed out, mixed in with other questions, and it was very obvious that she had done this many times before. She was recording the answers as soon as they were said or simultaneously when a reply was made.

Because I was so much at ease or because of her disarming ability, I responded, "I am a retired mercenary." I was more shocked than she was. I could not believe I said it. She flushed and the cool professional facade she had come in with, disappeared. We both looked at each other in disbelief. It was obvious she never expected that answer. I never had told anyone what I did. I didn't know what to do as I stood there looking at this little girl with brown hair and flashing eyes, as she was transformed into a chalk-white zombie.

"Didn't you ever meet one before?" I said in a jokingly fashion. "Did you expect horns growing out of our heads or something like that?"

Her color came back to her and she could just about mumble an "okay."

The questions continued about my general health and medicine that I was taking. More importantly, she changed. I didn't know how or why, but I felt she wasn't the same person who came into the room. At first I thought I was imagining it. She was standing right next to me and yet, I felt as though someone took her place. I must have reacted in a visible way because she stepped back. Silence became the third person in the room, a type of silence that both of us felt uncomfortable with but it was present all the same.

I got up to leave since I was starting to feel embarrassed sitting there. Nothing else was said as I picked up my jacket and started to leave.

"Do you have any questions?" she asked.

"Could what I have caused me to hallucinate?" I asked.

"I don't know," was the quivering response. "I don't know!"

"I'll need to see you again. I mean, we have to take your blood." She stammered as she spoke and led me toward another little room in which a man sat with all the equipment necessary for blood; a little rubber hose and a needle. By the time we got to the room, she had regained her composure and the professionalism came back into her voice. I was amazed how she could shift from one character to another so quickly. "See you in two weeks," she mumbled as she quickly moved away. "And take the pills I have prescribed for you."

"I can't come, I have to go to Vegas," I replied. "If all you need is blood, I can have a test made out there and mail it to you. Or better yet, they can fax it. You have a fax machine here, don't you?" My suggestion threw her. Like most doctors she could not handle the fact that I wanted to change her agenda.

"If I give you blood today, I'll call you and if you want to change anything you can tell me over the phone rather than me having to come here." Before she could say anything I continued. "If I die, I die."

"Fine," she said as she turned and started to disappear into one of the little rooms.

"Feeling a little bit better?" The blood man inquired with a grin on his face.

"A point well taken," I said. "I'll be here in two weeks!" I shouted after her.

For the next two weeks I was the best patient in the world. I took my pills religiously. Fields called every day. After he asked how I was he would go into great details with regard to the arrangements he made for me in Las Vegas. During the two weeks, as if by magic, the symptoms I had were disappearing. By the end of the two weeks whatever I had was under control and I felt good again. I showed up at the clinic on time. I was led into one of the little rooms and awaited my little angel of mercy. When she walked in, she knew I felt better.

"Are you going to laugh at me again?" she asked.

"No! I'm just going to sit here and wonder why, at this stage of my life, God sent me an angel," I replied. She went about the business of reading charts, looking at me and reading off a list of questions. She was finally done. Before she could speak, I said, "Doctor, whatever I say to you is covered by the doctor patient privilege; do you know that? I have to know whether or not my body will let me down because I have a job to do."

She looked at me as though she was afraid to answer.

"You've given me back the ability to do what I do; now I want to know whether or not I can." She stood there in the little room looking as though a great weight was placed on her. When she was talking about medicine she had an air about her that made her feel comfortable with her decisions. She was having trouble telling someone that they could "return to work" even though she had done it many times before…this time she didn't like the work.

After what seemed an eternity she mumbled, "Yes, but be careful."

"Why doctor?" I responded. "That is the first time you said something that didn't involve a body function or fluid!"

She smiled and started to leave the room. "Three months, see you in three months." She reached out to shake my hand good-bye, and when I touched her…her hands were soft…and the texture of her skin, extremely pleasant to the touch. I pulled her to me and we stood in the little room right next to each other. I felt embarrassed for touching her and as we stood there looking at each other my hands started to tremble. I was shocked by my own reaction and finally let go of her. She stared at me for a moment longer, and turned to leave, but turned to face me again.

"I still don't know if your condition would cause you to hallucinate...I'll keep researching it and when I find out, I'll call you...but I'll see you in three months...right?"

I nodded "yes."

# Chapter Nine

Receiving a clean bill of health I called Fields to tell him I was ready for Vegas. I had decided to go by train. It's a four-day trip and I thought being alone and away would not do me any harm. I had been given the necessary information about the people to see when I got there so I was set to go. I called Russ and asked him to come out. I didn't know what I would run into and, anyway, he was good company. I made arrangements for him to fly out and got him a room at the Tropicana. I called Tony and told him to be there.

The route of the train is from New York to Chicago. In Chicago I had to change trains for the trip through the mountains to Union Station in downtown Las Vegas. I was determined to enjoy the ride so I packed away all my negative thoughts and boarded the train in New York for the overnight trip to Chicago. There were very few people on the train, so I had most of the car to myself. As the train sped on, I fell into never-never land mentally. I was asleep and awake at the same time. Suddenly, I felt someone or something reaching out for me. I jumped up but no one was around. The other people in the car were all asleep and at least 15 seats away. I sat back down and as I settled in, there was the feeling of being called again. I sat there trying first to define what was happening since I felt ridiculous for having a feeling I couldn't describe.

As I looked out the window, the passing lights, sights of the countryside and small towns were hypnotizing me. Every so often the train would stop and I would race to get off the train for a moment since all of a sudden I couldn't breathe while I was on the train. At one point, I was just going to get off and stay a few days, but convinced myself that I was having a nightmare which I assumed was the evil side of a dream.

I sat down in my seat again as the train picked up speed. The noise from the wheels became a drum that beat out a message I couldn't understand. It was as though someone were talking in a foreign language, but saying the same thing over and over. The windows that first had provided a movie picture typesetting now became flash cards I was afraid to look at. My life was passing before me as though I had been an observer rather than a participant. I felt all alone. My thoughts were those of another, not my own memories, but rather like watching a movie one frame at a time, with no continuity but a series of snap shots. I had felt this loneliness one other time. It was years ago on my way back from a high school reunion. Try as I might, I couldn't shake the thought or the feeling while I was sitting on this train going to Las Vegas to meet people who many felt were not nice. For a mature man, I was acting like a teenager, or younger, but no matter how I tried to ridicule myself, the memories flashed back as the train whistled through the night. That same sick feeling was on me again. I jumped out of my seat and started walking the length of the train.

The rhythmic beating of the wheels of the train replaced the sound of the waves beating on the shore. The blackness outside intensified as the interior lights of the train were shut off. The passengers around me, one by one, slipped off to sleep. The air in the train picked up in velocity as it encircled the interior of the car in an endless search to find its way out. I found myself back on the beach in the south of Italy staring out into the Mediterranean.

I kept telling myself I was on a train going to Las Vegas. There were people around me.

No matter what I thought, the empty feeling of loneliness overcame me. I was all alone. I suddenly realized that loneliness could come at any time. The feeling is independent of the people in the room or the circumstances which surround it. It is an all encompassing feeling that blocks all forms of communication. It was like being in a plastic bubble in the middle of the room. Things were going on around me but I couldn't interact with any of them. I realized the cause is unknown and can be triggered by anything. It's a feeling of worthlessness when all of a sudden nothing means anything anymore. There was nothing. I was in a freefall with nothing to hang on to. What's even worse, I didn't care to save myself. The question of "Why should I?" had no answer. The world became a strange place in which all the familiar touchstones were gone. The hurt was inside so no one could help. No one could tell I was under the terrible spell of this insidious captor. So quickly did it strike that within the blink of an eye I was under its spell. The hurt from the loneliness beast was so deep that it paralyzed my whole being. But somehow the biggest fear was that I would break free. The windows acted as a mirror, but now they were not reflecting anything. After the first encounter, when I was sure I would be able to deal with the monster, when it reappeared I found myself as unsure of myself as I was before. I had gained no knowledge from my first experience. The brave façade wasn't working. I was as frightened as I was before. It seemed that the more I tried to understand what was happening the more confused I got. The answer had to be with Betsy if she were still alive. The realization that this whole thing, which I didn't understand might be caused by some supernatural being became mind-boggling. I had to find her no matter what. I was on my way to Vegas and I couldn't rid her from my thoughts. She was alive and well. I knew she had to be. Russ would help. She's out there somewhere. I just knew it. Sleep became my unsolicited ally. I embraced it

Four days later, the train finally pulled into Union Station, Las Vegas. It was the longest four days, and even longer four nights of my life. As I got off, there was Russ, smiling as usual. When he saw me, he ran over to help me with my bags.

"You look horrible, what did you do, pull the train here?"

When I didn't react, he turned around and stopped. "What's the matter? Are you still sick? You're okay?" He fired the questions faster than I could answer.

"Russ, when this is over, you have to help me find someone. You know everybody and everything. Will you help?" Before he could answer, I walked out the door and hailed a cab. The cabby loaded the baggage and we were off.

If there ever were a place to forget everything, it's Las Vegas. The route from downtown to the Tropicana goes right down the strip. The hotels pass with an array of color, lights, and advertisements. There is a never-ending flow of people, cars, and buses, but I couldn't get my mind off her. I guess it showed because when we got to the room, Russ grabbed the bags from the bellman, and threw them on the bed.

"George," he said, "you'd better get your head on straight. The pills are here. They want..."

Before he finished, I asked him again, "Will you help? Call some of the people you know and let's get started."

Russ turned toward me and hesitated a moment. "George, I can't explain what is happening to you, or why, but I do know that whatever it is you had better get rid of it and concentrate on what is happening here."

I told Russ the story of what was happening to me. I didn't give him all the details since they embarrassed me.

In a compassionate voice he said, "What you're seeing or feeling is based on a memory or whatever that is over forty-years-old. Why now? These memories that are haunting you are weird...but that's all it is, weird. Don't read into what is happening, something that doesn't exist...or better still, re-examine what you're feeling. Maybe you're better off just leaving well enough alone. You only remember...you know...you only remember what you want to remember, and in your case, there is nothing to remember. I know what I said doesn't make much sense, but...well...you are a logical person, that's why people have hired you. You can see the answer before most people know there is a problem. Now you're trying to deal with an emotional experience...man...I don't think you know how to, and that's what's bugging you. For the first time you think you know what love is...but it's not...for the first time in your life you're reaching for something...but it isn't there...I know, by now you had given up any hope of finding or feeling such an emotion...let this lady go...be happy with the fact you now know that the emotion exists...you're going to go nuts over this...I don't even know what 'this' is...you got me nuts."

"Well, thank you," I said. "I'm glad to hear that's what you think of me...I mean, what can I say? Thank you." I sat on the nearest thing to me and looked at Russ in disbelief.

Russ was ashamed of what he had said and was at a loss for words. He moved around the room as the both of us sat in silence. I got up and started to leave the room when Russ continued.

"George, I didn't mean to insult you, but you have to think about what you're saying."

"Russ," I said in a low voice. "I have thought about what is happening...the trouble is I don't know what it is. I know what I saw in Italy, I know what I felt on the train. I'm so goddamn smart I know everything...everything. Don't I sound like I know everything?"

Russ looked amazed. "I'll help! I'll do it. First let's get this over with. We are to have dinner in the hotel. I've reserved a private dining room. We will be able to talk and be finished with this. When we get home, we'll find her! What are you going to do if she doesn't want to be found?" His voice dropped to a whisper. "Better yet," he said with a renewed vigor, "why don't you write her a letter?"

"Get out," I said. "Let me go to sleep. We'll meet at seven o'clock. Dinner's here in the hotel! Okay?"

Russ left and sleep was the agenda for at least a couple of

hours. I left word with the desk to be called at six p.m. and laid down. Fields had told me they wanted $60,000 for the six pills. The pills had been sent to a druggist in Las Vegas, but that was all I was told. I didn't know how the pills were found and I really didn't care. The pills were identified by the watermark on the box. The problem was that a chemist would have to run a test to see if the pills in the box were the ones we were looking for. A rumor was started that the pills may not be from the batch but rather made up just for the money. A chemical analysis had to be made to be sure. Russ had made contact with a local chemist who would be joining us for dinner and he would do the testing.

At 7 p.m. I met Russ. He and I were the first two in the private room. It was a regular suite with the beds removed and a long table put in. It was set for six people. A full-length mirror was on the door that led to the bathroom. Drapes were over the windows, which we checked to make sure they were locked. A service table was against one wall. The problem was, my mind wasn't on the problem at hand and it must have shown.

Russ was visibly upset. "George, snap out of it, I'll find her, I swear. Now come on, wake up! I told Tony to be nearby in case we need him."

I smiled and turned just in time to greet the waiter who was starting to bring in the menus for dinner. Within minutes, the chemist arrived. He brought the necessary equipment to set up a mini laboratory for testing the pills. Directly behind him was the druggist who found the pills and two men who tried very hard to act like bodyguards. They walked all around the room...trying other doors that were in the room to see if they were locked. Satisfied, everyone sat down to order. Everybody was there. After the normal greetings and ordering of dinner, the waiter left. I motioned for Russ to leave and take the chemist with him.

"Gentlemen," I started. "As far as I know, the deal has been made and my job is to check out the goods and pay you or, in the alternative, take the pills and not give you anything." The three men looked at each other in shock. They expected anything but this. I stood up and quietly poured some wine that the waiter had brought in, and asked if anyone else wanted some.

The three men were stunned by what I had just said and hook their heads, "No."

"I am supposed to pay you fifty thousand for six pills." I went on. The eldest of the men started to stand but I motioned for him to stay seated.

"Sixty thousand," he said.

"Sixty or there is no deal," he said again in a louder voice.

"You're right, but that means I don't get anything," I replied as I took a sip of wine.

"You'll get fifty thousand, I'll get ten thousand or you won't leave this room. Now take your time and let's have dinner." I went into the hall and motioned for Russ and the chemist to come back in. My timing was perfect. The waiter was there with the food. I first introduced everyone and then told them my plan for dinner and for testing the pills. Russ made a few jokes and dinner proceeded without a hitch.

Dinner was filled with idle chatter covering topics ranging from sports to politics. The waiter reappeared at exactly the right moments to bring coffee and clear the table. The chatter continued through coffee.

After dinner, the older man, along with his renewed demand for 60,000, produced a box. Fields had warned me that they might try to re-negotiate at the last minute.

"You have to stand your ground!" Fields shouted over the phone.

"Why don't you come here or send one of your people and I'll leave?" I snapped back. "I rode that God damn train here, I feel like shit. I was trying to sleep and you've got to call me with this bullshit." Fields lowered his voice to the point that I couldn't hear him.

"What did you say?" I yelled into the phone.

"I've instructed the manager to give you seventy-five thousand in credit," Fields said.

"Credit? Are you nuts? Do you really expect me to gamble? Get the cash up here before I meet with them. I'll take care of the rest. That's why you have me here, remember?" I hung up.

Just before 7 p.m., the money was delivered to me. I divided it into four envelopes. Two envelopes contained $25,000 each; one contained $15,000 and the last one $10,000.

I looked at the box, turned to the chemist and asked, "How long to test these?"

"A few minutes," was the response.

"Give him the pills," I said to the men. "Here's twenty-five thousand to count." I handed over the first envelope. I then took out the other envelope with the other $25,000 in it. I turned just enough so that they could see the other envelope with $10,000 marked on it. The table was still covered with the coffee dishes. They had to be removed for the chemist to spread out his testing equipment. I motioned to him to set up on the service table. The chemist complied. He tested the pills and nodded his approval. I handed over the other envelope and motioned for the chemist to leave. Although when he came, everything in his kit was neatly placed, he just grabbed up everything and left. The waiter started to come in but one of the other men went to the door and motioned for him to leave. He shut the door and locked it.

One of Russ's greatest assets was his sense for guessing when something bad was going to happen. He often was called Radar after the character on M*A*S*H. He went to the far side of the room. One nice thing about Russ was that you never could rely on him. It was really an asset. When he was with you; you never had to guess what he would do. You knew that he would be no help at all.

I had the pills in my pocket; one man was by the door, the older man was across from me with the two envelopes in his hand, the third man stood up and was starting to move around the table, saying, "We're not leaving without the other ten thousand dollars."

Russ yelled, "Hey Rube."

The door came crashing in. In one motion, Tony picked up the dining table and threw it at the two men. Before leaving for the meeting I had told Russ to tell Tony to be close. "Tell him to keep in touch with the waiter. The waiter will be able to tell him what's happening. We'll yell when we want him to join us." Tony had proven invaluable to me in the restaurant with Mr. Fields, and I knew his unique service would be needed again. Whacking is a fading art...I knew that whacking would be needed here and as far as I was concerned, Tony was the best. The waiter had told him that one of the men had locked the door behind him. Tony waited for the call.

The man by the door rebounded off the wall but took one look at Tony and left. Russ was yelling, "I love it, don't give up, get him, I love it!"

Tony left, half chasing the man down the hall. Just as Tony went through the door he looked back and I waved him off. The other two men started to move, trying to sweep the glass from the mirror off themselves. When they had fallen, they had hit the mirror on the bathroom door and shattered it. The glass was all over them. The waiter, hearing the noise, came back in the room and looked in disbelief. Russ tiptoed around the table and men, still laughing and shouting, "You're beautiful George! You are a work of art!"

I took some money out of my pocket, paid the bill and gave the waiter a generous tip. "Clean up the mess; keep your mouth shut. Bill him for the damage if there is any." As I spoke I was pointing to one of the men on the floor. I gave the waiter some more money.

The waiter shook his head and stuttered out the words, "I'll fix it."

Russ and I went to my room. "That was just great," Russ said. "Just great, I loved it. Are you taking the Choo-Choo back?"

"I'm flying with you," I said. "Get us on the next plane." Russ kept walking around the room describing what happened, re-enacting certain portions of it, jumping from the sofa to table and back to the sofa. He was just being a damn nuisance.

The phone rang. Russ picked up the phone and said his infamous, "Yeess." It was for him. The coloration of his face started to change, but with Russ you didn't know whether it was natural or he was faking it. I was starting to get changed since I was a mess. The sauces and oil or whatever they were, were all over my suit. Looking at myself in the mirror, I couldn't for the life of me figure out how I got so messed up; but most of all, I was thinking about my new quest...I had to find her. The bad part was I didn't know why. I could not recall any events or conversations that would cause me to have these memories which really didn't make any sense at all, nor could I recall any basis for them.

In school, Betsy went her way and I had gone mine. Both our last names started with the same last letter, and that fact alone determined the class we were in and where we sat in class since it was usually done alphabetically. We were in the same classes for six years going from grades seven through 12. In the four years of high school, she was in the college group and I was in the general group. That meant I was destined to be expelled from school at any time. I was always very strong, even as a freshman; the older boys bothered someone other than me. I would prefer to have lunch alone than be with the in-crowd. There used to be a joke to describe my attitude, "The only way he'll say anything is if you choke him and then he'll just ask you to lighten up your grip," which of course, was never said to me. The teachers passed me because the thought of having me around for another year was more than they could take. It seemed that they would have a meeting, decide what grades were needed to pass me, and do it.

While working with my father one weekend, I was hit in the eye with a piece of steel. There was great concern by the doctors that I might lose my sight. That changed my life and attitude. After an operation and missing six weeks of school, I was allowed to return but had to wear sunglasses all the time. I was excused from my classes every two hours to go to the nurse to have drops put into my eye. The class day ran from 9 a.m. to 3:30 p.m. and normally, students would have seven classes a day. If the students weren't in a class they sat in a study hall which meant they sat staring into a book to keep the study hall monitor from bothering them. Since my reading had to be limited, by doctor's orders, study halls were out. Also, I couldn't take gym since any physical contact or strenuous exercise was not allowed. The principal called me to his office and told me, "You will be excused from study halls and gym. By rearranging your classes, you can be out by one fifteen every day. However, you have to maintain a B average. Is it a deal?"

I nodded "yes."

That one phrase changed me. I couldn't study for a B. If I didn't study I would get Ds, and pass, if I studied, I would get an A. During my junior and senior year I was a good student. My guidance counselor started to talk to me about furthering my education. My classes were changed so that I went with the smart kids. Up to this point, I never had a math class. In my senior year, after fulfilling my required classes, I took algebra. Algebra was a freshman class which meant I was the only senior in a freshman class. There was some concern as to how disruptive that would be. I assured everyone that everything would be okay.

The first day of class I got there early. I grabbed the two

biggest kids in the class, and, in front of everyone else, banged their heads together. I never said a word. I sat down, and there never were any disturbances in that class. The teacher would teach and leave, congratulating himself on how well he ran the class. He never knew why until years later when one of the students told him. The problem was that algebra was hard to understand, so if I had a book or was reading a book, it was algebra. Betsy saw me and said, "If you need any help, I'll help you." And she did. Whenever I got into trouble, I would go to her, and she would stop what she was doing and answer my questions. That was it. The questions became fewer as I caught onto algebra. I got a perfect final test, which I showed to Betsy. That was the sum total of involvement and conversations with this woman who was now driving me nuts.

"George, George, do you hear me?" Russ was now yelling. "What the hell is it with you? Wake up! What are you doing, still thinking about that bitch? Those three guys are in a room figuring out what to do with you and you're daydreaming about someone who doesn't even know you're alive. What's the matter with you? You better..."

I got up, re-buttoned and zipped everything I had unbuttoned and unzipped. "What's their room number?"

Before Russ could answer..."Get us on the next plane...How do you know what they're doing?"

Russ smiled. "Spies man, spies," he said as he went into a little dance. He told me the number. I picked up an ashtray and went down the hallway, and knocked on one of the doors.

"Tony, are you there?"

"Yes."

"Come on," I said. Within a few minutes, Tony walked out of the room. By now, I was down the hallway. I turned and saw Tony behind me. "Room six thousand and eleven!" I yelled. Tony nodded, and we went our separate ways.

At room 601, I knocked politely on the door. I heard,

"Who's there?" I didn't answer. One of the trio opened the door. He was more engrossed in the conversation he was having with the other two men and did not look to see who was at the door. I dropped the ashtray in place. I stepped in, but was careful not to shut the door. There wasn't a sound in the room; the three men stared at me.

"You have all your parts," I started. "Plus, fifty thousand dollars. You have this day, made a nice profit and are able to enjoy it. This thing ends now. If you let it fester, you will not have any money...You will not be able to enjoy it...And some of your parts won't be working or else will be missing...It ends here and now...If not, tell me now, and I will deal with it."

The three men looked at each other, half in disbelief and half in shock. There I was, with a messed up suit and shirt with stains all over them. I was standing in the room, but away from the three men, talking to them in a conversational tone as though I were addressing a class of some sort. They took notice that somehow I had managed to keep the door ajar, since it hadn't entirely closed. They couldn't see the ashtray I had dropped and kicked into place. The three men were in a group, and now started to spread out. The oldest of the three took one step forward.

"You son-of-a-bitch...Who the hell..." Before he said anything else, the door was kicked open. It hit the back wall, bounced back and Tony hit and kicked it simultaneously. The door split. The three men stared in disbelief.

The center man, without taking his eyes off of Tony, was half yelling, "It's over, Man, it's over!"

I turned to leave. Tony had to move the pieces of the door before I could get out. I half stepped back in, took out some money...counted out five $100 bills, and threw it at them. "Fix the door." Tony and I left. I went north and Tony south.

As the elevator door opened, two security guards got off and ran down the hallway toward 601. I waited until they got there and could hear, "It's okay".

I heard someone say, "It was just an accident."

When I got back to the room, Russ was on the phone laughing and shouting, "I love it...I love it!" When I came in, he hung up. Still laughing he said, "Spies man, spies." He knew everything that had happened. "Our plane leaves in an hour!" he shouted as he was leaving. "In the lobby, in a half hour, and take off those clothes, they stink."

I looked at myself in the mirror. I was a sight to behold. I undressed, dressed and packed by throwing everything into my suitcase, except the suit and shirt. "Mr. Fields better give me another one," I said half aloud, while I threw the suit and shirt into the garbage. Russ was in the lobby waiting, and had already made arrangements for transportation to the airport.

"Your property damage bill was more than the hotel bill I bet," Russ said as he laughed to himself.

The ride home was uneventful, except for Russ moving his seat. "Sitting next to him is like nothing else I've ever experienced," Russ told the stewardess as he pointed to me. Russ went with the stewardess. I sat back in the seat, trying to sleep, while at the same time, trying to remember, but unfortunately there was nothing to remember except the intermittent thoughts I had of her. This fact alone infuriated me even more. I settled back and resolved, I must be nuts.

I felt my pocket for the six pills. The two envelopes containing the $15,000 and $10,000, I had packed in my suitcase. Although Fields had said pay them 60, I paid 50 and charged Fields 15 for going. I felt I did a good job and looked upon the 10 as a bonus, or tip. I finally drifted off, hearing Russ's laughter way off in the background.

# Chapter Ten

Upon arriving home, I was determined to find the reason for my dreams, visions, or nightmares. By this time, what used to be a nightmare would be called daydreaming? It was as though I drifted off into outer space. Someone coming into my office would bring me back to reality. Their entrance was usually met with a harsh remark. "What the hell are you bothering me for?" was a favorite.

The search consisted of calling everyone I knew, or whom I thought knew Betsy. They were contacted, and asked to contact someone else, etc. Russ was given the project of searching official records. The problem, of course, was being the age of the records and the reluctance of people to divulge privileged information. Of course, both the obstacles were overcome. Within a few days, she was located.

"We found her," Russ proudly announced as he came triumphantly marching into my office. I did not tell him that I, through my own efforts, succeeded as well.

Just to be on the safe side I asked, "What's her phone number?"

Russ responded. The numbers he gave me were the same as I had and that made me more confident that they were correct.

"All right, let's go," I said, as I grabbed a jacket, and started toward the door. Russ, for the first time, wasn't smiling, nor making any jokes.

"Wait!" he yelled. "Where the hell are you going? Are you nuts? Calm down!"

From the tone and volume of Russ's voice, I was taken back, and the only word I could formulate was "Why?" which was said in a sheepish, childlike manner.

"Look at yourself," Russ commanded. "You're a throwback

to the Stone Age…calm down…wait a week. This way you'll calm down and have time to think this thing through." I was astounded by Russ's words of caution and his unwillingness for immediate and direct action.

"I don't believe you," I started. "After all the things we've been through together, you're afraid to go see some old woman? What did you say she did?"

"School teacher," Russ interrupted. "A skinny school teacher" He continued. "George, look, here are pictures of other women I know, look, three twenties or two thirties, why do you want to find this one?"

"Russ," I half shouted. "If you're afraid, stay home, and I'll go myself. I can't believe you want me to wait a week! Let's go. We can be there in two hours! What are you afraid of?"

"Of you!" Russ shouted back. Again there were no jokes, no dancing but rather a totally out of character Russ. "Look at yourself. You're too deep into this. Whatever you're remembering is over forty-years-old, what you find may be nothing like what you're remembering. Maybe you better just keep your memories, or whatever, and leave reality alone…this isn't a job anymore. It has become very personal to you…I have never seen you like this. A week's wait isn't going to change anything except it may give you some time to think things out. It's become a…"

Before he could finish, I had stopped, turned around and went to one of the chairs in the room, not to sit on, but to merely lean against. The rest of Russ's words seemed to drift into space as I thought back to the Cardinal I had gone to see, unbeknown to Russ.

I remembered the advice he had given me that I should talk to my local priest about what I was experiencing. I thought to myself, my friend, who is a priest, is more messed up than I am, but I remembered him mentioning the Monsignor from Saint Peter's Church. I had spoken to the Monsignor once when I wanted to see if there was any information about Betsy at the church. He had informed me that such information is confidential to the church. I just accepted his ridiculous answer and didn't press the issue. I recall thinking that he is confused as to who the church is. I would bet that he would still vote for the Latin mass. I didn't want to dwell on his response, and, also recalled that anyone I spoke to about him thought he was a "nice and understanding" priest. That was good enough for me. In addition to his duties at St. Peter's, he also had some sort of function at the Archdiocese of Newark. He had an office in downtown Newark as well as one at St. Peter's. I felt he doesn't know me; really doesn't know Betsy and, in theory anyway, he is something more than a parish priest. I decided to call him and set up a luncheon or dinner meeting.

It took a couple of calls, but I finally reached him. I felt rather awkward, even talking to him, but I persevered. He sounded annoyed at first, but settled down and listened, as I rambled on about making an appointment and suggested a luncheon or a dinner meeting. I was holding my breath, waiting for a response, because I really didn't want to meet him in an office setting or in a church. I now think back and realize how silly that was. I was relieved when he said he could meet that Thursday evening for dinner. I told him I would pick him up at the rectory and he expressed concern for his safety. Before he could finish the sentence, I just started to laugh. I tried to stop myself, but before I could, it was as though someone else were speaking. I told him that it was the second time that I had been accused of being from the Stone Age. He didn't know what I was talking about, but I told him I would meet him anytime, anywhere, under his terms and conditions, except that it was my treat. He sounded more relaxed, and he agreed to meet me. I told him about a restaurant in Harrison, El Mason, I thought he would enjoy. He agreed, and on that Thursday, I went to pick him up.

When I pulled up to the rectory, there was a priest standing in front of it and for the first time, I realized that all the priests looked the same way, hunched over shoulders, and portly physique. He was a little shorter than I and was busily chatting with some elderly woman. I made my driver pull up in front of the rectory and I got out. The women and the priest both stared in bewilderment at the limo. I felt ridiculous...why did I rent that car? My embarrassment must have shown, but the good priest just smiled and extended his hand to greet me. "You must be George."

Before I could say anything, he turned to the woman to say good-bye but she wasn't paying attention to him as she was bending over to peer into the limo. He got in and slid over for me to get in. I quickly explained to him that the reason I was using the car was that we were going to dinner, I would probably have wine, and that a DWI charge against me would exceed the cost of using the car. The rest of the journey to the restaurant was filled with idle chatter as we compared notes as to people we knew and places we had been. We finally arrived at the restaurant.

The Maître D' recognized me since I had been there many times, and motioned me to the table he knew I liked, which was in the corner facing the rest of the dining room. The Monsignor was visibly impressed. "You must come here a lot," he said. I didn't respond, but walked over and sat down. We set about the task of ordering our dinner and wine. After that was accomplished, his priestly training and experience came through.

"Normally, I would say, 'And what is troubling you, my son,' but since you're older than I, I'll just call you?"

I interjected, "George."

He seemed satisfied with that as he added, "Why don't you tell me what is on your mind and in your heart. You look like you're carrying a great burden."

I started to tell him my tale of woe. I started with the trip up the Hudson, and continued with the incident at Saratoga. When I got to the sighting in Italy, I could see I definitely had his attention. Within a few minutes after telling him the story, I felt completely relaxed and, after the first glass of wine, I felt even more relaxed. The only time he interrupted me was to have me say grace. I talked through the appetizers, dinner, and by the time we got to coffee, the wine was finished. He just sat there, interjecting a question here and there to better understand what I was saying or to better understand the story I was relating. When I finally shut up, he sat back in the chair, took a long look at me and said something brilliant like, "This experience has really unnerved you?" I didn't respond because I never expected that response.

Why did he think I called him and took him out to dinner; for the hell of it? I was thinking to myself. But my disappointment in his first statement must have been written on my face because he continued. "I have heard stories and have read the same books you have about one person being able to sense the feelings of another...But this is the first time I've ever come face to face with it. I obviously don't know the answer and really don't have a Saint readily available for you to pray to."

He half laughed after the last comment, and I am sure he said it to relax me more than for any other reason. By now, my hands were actually shaking. He noticed it also and saw how embarrassed I was when I realized it. I quickly put my hands in my lap. The waiter came over and took our coffee order and left.

He started to ramble on, but I just couldn't make any sense out of what he was saying. He hesitated talking until he was sure I was listening before he made the comment: "They must know that when you come here you want to be left alone. That waiter has kept everyone away from us and never came back during the meal to see if everything was all right…You know they usually do that when your mouth is full of food. I see it is not going to be easy for me to get you to relax but I sure wish you would. As you know, there is not going to be an easy answer, but with faith there will be an answer."

I was trying very hard to be consumed by his words, but instead found myself predicting what he would say next. Sure enough, the next words out of his mouth, as I had anticipated, were: "You should sit down and write a letter to her and to yourself. By putting your experiences on paper, you will be better able to deal with them. You might even want to reach out and meet with her to see if she can help you in any way."

As he was talking, I wanted to choke him. I swear I wanted to choke him. "Father," I said, "I would gladly call her. I would love to meet with her. I will tell her everything that I told you. The only immediate results may be that for the first time in a long time, I will sleep the whole night. I will be so proud of myself for accomplishing that much. I am, I guess, afraid that if I call her, she will not want to hear from me. What if she doesn't want to be bothered with me? She has made her own life up to now without me?"

As I rambled on, it was as though the priest wasn't there and I was reading the words from a blackboard wondering if, I could improve upon them.

The priest must have realized it too, because with a half smile he said, "I bet you can envision both sides of a conversation simultaneously."

His comment caught me off guard for the moment, but I reflected upon how I must have sounded, so I just nodded and continued drinking my coffee.

I finished my coffee, paid the bill and went outside and into the car for the ride home. These movements were done in motion completely oblivious to the priest. Once inside the car, he broke the silence. "Have you spoken to her?"

I heard the words, but it took me awhile to assimilate their meaning. "No," I said, almost shouting. "I wanted to so she could say more and I was hoping maybe she would continue the conversation and maybe she would, but if she didn't, I would hang up."

He acknowledged that he heard me by chuckling and smiling. We arrived back at the rectory, got out of the car, and in a mechanical way, shook his hand and I thanked him for coming.

He started to walk away, turned, and said, "I don't know your number...give me your card. Don't write me off so soon, let me think about this; when I was a young priest I had all the answers at my fingertips, but now that I am a Monsignor, it takes me longer. I will remember you in my prayers." I handed him my card. He took it as he waved and disappeared behind the front door. I went home.

In evaluating my own performance, I was disappointed in myself, but more importantly, I felt embarrassed even telling a complete stranger a story that I could not believe myself. I started to have doubts as to whether or not I went into too much detail or didn't tell him enough. I had omitted the numerous times I felt something was wrong in her life and quickly dismissed it as being foolish. I didn't tell him of other times when I had imagined I heard her, or saw her, only to find on closer examination that there was no one there. I couldn't help feeling how much easier life is when you can rationalize everything in terms of a God or some other divine power. One can just sit back and offer his sufferings up to God, the way they teach you in Sunday school or immediately drop to one's knees and pray, and by concentrating on the prayer completely eliminate all other thoughts from your mind.

Somehow, as I've gotten older, I look upon such behavior as a way out rather than a solution. I started to philosophize that if God didn't want me to deal with certain problems, I would not have been given the power to think; I would be void of all feelings and just be placed in a mental limbo. God must be testing my strength, but I never thought I would be put through this type of hell.

"George...George..." By now, Russ was screaming. "Goddamn! One week, Okay?"

I nodded, "Yes."

"Tomorrow you have a meeting with Fields at his New York apartment, don't you?"

Again I nodded "Yes."

"Okay," Russ responded and he left.

# Chapter Eleven

The next day Russ called and asked what time the meeting with Fields was and what I was doing afterwards. "Do you want me to come to the meeting with Fields?" he asked. "I'll drive you and wait for you!" I had never known Russ to be so accommodating.

"That wouldn't be necessary," I said. "I'll call you when I get done which should be about noon."

The words no sooner came out and he replied, "Great. I want you to go see someone." As an afterthought he yelled into the phone, "I had the place wired!" Before I could respond he hung up.

The meeting with Fields was in his New York apartment. I drove there myself and parked in the building and took the elevator up to the 16th floor. As I entered the apartment, it seemed changed somehow, but I didn't know how. The things all looked the same except for the wall to the right as I entered the room. It was all mirrors. The room looked gigantic. I looked at Fields sitting at the table. He was getting up to meet me. I waved for him to sit down. Fields looked ashen and under a lot of stress but was cordial in this demeanor. He motioned for me to sit so that my back was to the wall of mirrors. Fields never really got out of the chair nor did he leave the area of the table where he was seated. Fields started to ramble on about what had transpired with regard to the pills, how he and I had first met and all the incidents that had led up to today's meeting.

I sat there at first congratulating myself on a job well done, but realized that the speech I was hearing was coming from Fields, not a close, personal friend. It was as though Fields was giving a report in front of a class. The fact that I began to feel uneasy and started to squirm in the chair did not deter Fields from rambling on about the Italy incidents and the brilliant performance in Vegas. He added, "I figured out you wound up with twenty five thousand instead of the fifteen thousand we agreed to but that's all right, you were worth it." By now I was standing. Fields pressed something and a door opened on the opposite side of the room from the mirrors. The click of the lock startled me. Two servants walked in.

Fields immediately continued. "George, please sit down. I am having coffee and toast served. Would you like anything else? They can prepare anything else you want." I nodded "no" but didn't understand why two servants would be needed just to make coffee for two men. I started to walk around the room. The wall of mirrors kept attracting my attention, but I didn't know why.

"Come sit down and have your coffee," Mr. Fields insisted. When I came back to the table he motioned for the maid to move his place setting to the other side of the table so that he was now facing the wall. The maid poured the coffee and I watched to make sure the two coffees came from the same pot. The other maid poured the milk into Fields' cup. I motioned to her that I would pour my own. The two servants left. Fields busied himself with the table setting in front of him. I felt a tension building in the room but not from anything I could perceive through my five senses but something else was there. My sixth sense, ESP, was working overtime.

"Fields," I half shouted. "Why am I here?" The words came out more like a command rather than a question.

"For two reasons," Fields replied. "I want to try to talk you into another assignment and I want to give you a bonus. I remembered you commented on how you liked the older limo I had because you fit in it, so I had it redone." While he was talking, he handed me an envelope. The car had been registered in my name as noted on the registration form that was sticking out of the envelope. I finished opening the envelope and the bill of sale, the insurance card and policy were inside.

"The car is being delivered to your home as we speak. You can have the driver for today, but he's mine, so send him back." Fields stood up but did not move from the table. He extended his hand out to me. As I shook it, Fields in a very low voice said, "Thank you, you saved my life. Go and enjoy your car. I'll discuss the other matter another day."

Now I really was confused. I nodded and walked toward the door. When I opened it to leave, Fields shouted to me, "Did you find her yet? Can I help? If you need to use any of our facilities, just let me know." I looked back, smiled and half waved as I walked out the door and closed it behind me.

In the hallway I paused for a moment to reassess what had just transpired.

I had Tony follow me just in case. As I was leaving Tony approached me and after looking all around said, "Russ told you he had the place wired?"

I nodded "yes" but I wasn't really paying attention to what Tony was saying. I was still wondering how Fields knew about my search. Tony and I heard a whirling sound but we concluded it was an elevator.

"I'm going to leave. Call me later when you find out what is going on in that room today. Don't know why but I felt very uncomfortable in there."

Tony nodded his head "yes" and I went to the garage to get my car to hurry home to my limo. Just the thought of it made me smile. I thought back to my years after high school when I was in my own small business. If the boys could see me now!

Tony went into a door that led to the kitchen area of the apartment. The two waitresses met him and led him to where the recording device had been placed. The ladies were in on the snooping that would be going on. Tony looked into the room and was surprised to see the activity going on. The whirling sound we had heard was not an elevator but rather the motor needed to completely open the mirrored wall so that the room I was in and the next room became one. Seated in a semi-circle around a circular table in the center of the room were five men. Fields got up from his chair and walked over to the group. One of the gentlemen pushed a button and a maid's head appeared.

"You can serve now," he said. The men moved their chairs evenly around the table while the two maids hurriedly set the place settings.

"Can you give me ten minutes?" Fields asked almost apologetically. The maids nodded and both of them scurried out of the room.

"They are the steering committee for the company. They decide the overall strategy to take in meeting companywide problems," one of the maids told Tony. Tony double-checked the recorder for he wanted to make sure he got everything down for his report to George.

"Well, gentlemen, we have all seen Mr. George, and have been briefed as to what transpired and the results achieved." He stated these words as though he were a general about to lead his troops into battle. "We now have to decide Mr. George's future. We can vote now or observe him for a while longer before we decide. Does anyone have anything to say? Should we have a discussion or brunch?" He said with a half smile.

One of the other men first looked around the table, but seeing no one else wanted to speak, said in a very quiet tone, "We'd better take our time on this one. George accomplished all we asked him to and in a very quiet fashion. He may be a fine addition to our group. We are certainly in…"

Before he could finish, Fields interrupted. "No." Fields got up, visibly annoyed and walked to the other room. "No," he replied again. The door to the kitchen area opened again and the maids came out with the food. The group sat quietly and looked at each other.

One of them said, "We'll wait a while," and began to taste

the different items being served. It was very obvious to Tony that the group wanted Fields to leave.

Fields, still annoyed, said, "I have to leave. I'll call you later." His comment was directed towards one of the men who nodded his approval. Fields called for his car and his bodyguard who was in another room. The guard came in to the room and stood by Fields' side. Fields motioned to his bodyguard to leave. The guard reached down, put his four and a half fingers around the knob and the two men left.

On the ride back, I became more intrigued on how Fields knew I was looking for Betsy. The thought of the limo took over my thoughts. When I arrived home, there was a blue limo parked in front of my house and there was Russ talking to the driver. I pulled my car into the driveway. Russ came walking up the driveway. "All right, all right," he said. "You sure know how to please a customer. Come on, let's go."

"Where the hell are we going?" I asked. "Let me go inside for a minute."

Russ nodded and walked back down the driveway. "All right, I'll be in the car...I love it."

I went into the house for a few minutes as the phone was ringing. It was Tony and he started telling me in detail about the wall that moved and the five-member steering committee. "Fields got mad when one of them started to talk about keeping you around. He stomped out of the room like a little kid."

I told Tony to stay with it and check in with me later. I left my house from the front door and walked over to the car which was running. I went over to it, opened the door and got in. There was Russ with the TV on, sitting back sipping a drink. "I love it," he kept saying. "Here, have a drink. It's only soda." He handed me a glass. "On, James!" he shouted. "His name isn't James, but what the hell."

"Do you mind if I know where we are going?" I asked.

"You'll see," Russ responded as he was fiddling with the

TV. Finally, he shut it off. "I love it!" he shouted again.

"Russ, where are we going?" I was more insistent now.

"You, my dear friend, business associate of many years, and modern day love struck senior citizen, you are going to see a psychic. I've gotten directions and made all the arrangements. You'll love it."

I looked in disbelief. "Stop the car! Are you nuts? Stop the goddamn car!" The driver complied and pulled to the curb awaiting further instructions. I had turned into some sort of mad man who didn't know what to do next.

Russ just kept on talking. "Do you have a better idea? Have you ever been to a psychic? Do you have a better idea? Drive on, James and don't listen to this mad man…Drive on so that we can locate the source of this poor man's infliction. Drive on!"

"I ought to choke the shit out of you," I responded.

Russ, completely oblivious to my threat, continued. "A trip to the psychic is an experience and like any new experience, it is to be enjoyed or if not enjoyed, at least given the opportunity to be enjoyed.

She, the psychic, was located about an hour's drive from my house, so getting there gave me a lot of time to reflect why I was going, but even more important, I was determined that I would not give any clue as to why I was going.

After making all the necessary rights and lefts, we entered the apartment complex where she lived. All the buildings were two stories high and the buildings were lettered. Try as we may, we could not locate her apartment. Desperately, Russ used the portable phone and called her. As it turned out, we were in the wrong section. For some reason unbeknownst to anyone, two buildings had the same address. She gave the driver more directions to her apartment and said she would wait outside for us. The "new" directions were followed and we were in the right area in a minute or two. As we approached the parking area designated for the building this woman appeared in her shorts and sweatshirt. Both items were too big for her even though she was quite fleshy.

She motioned for us to park the car, which we did and I got out and followed her to the apartment. It was the typical small garden type apartment with small rooms and little windows that let in enough light to make the room appear mystic. The room was a mess. There were baseball caps all over the place, books, papers, and other debris thrown around. In the archway between the living room and the dining room was a card table with a lamp on it. The walls were covered with photographs of different family events or at least that was the impression I got. She motioned for me to sit at the table but I kept looking around. Finally I sat in the chair she had cleaned off for me.

"Is your friend joining us?" she asked as she busied herself arranging the items on the table, which now consisted of a lamp, ashtray and deck of cards.

"No," I replied as I settled back into my chair.

She picked up the deck of cards and shuffled them. She spread them in front of me, asked me to select 15 cards, put them in a pile, make a wish and give the cards to her. She turned them over, one at a time, and made three rows of five cards each. The three cards that caught her attention the most were a pair of kings and the Queen of Spades. She spoke in broad descriptive terms and said things that one would expect just by seeing me in a limo. She interjected about my health, my high blood pressure, etc. This amused me only because on the drive down, I had laid out in my mind what she would say and I felt proud that I was so accurate with my predictions. I was just about to halt the reading, pay her and leave when again she referred to the pair of kings. She pointed and said, "This one's a doctor, but the other one isn't the same kind of doctor...No, he's a psychiatrist...a psychiatrist and a doctor, that's what I see."

She said nothing about the Queen of Spades. I was just about to ask her about them when she quickly scooped up all the cards and had me repeat the process, only this time with nine cards. She again arranged them in rows but this time, three cards to a row. The pair of kings appeared again. I couldn't remember if they were the same two but while she was talking I was trying to calculate the odds of getting a pair of kings two hands in a row. She now became adamant that she saw me with a doctor and a psychiatrist...her expression changed. When I had first sat down, she had asked me if I wanted to hear the good and the bad, or just the good.

I responded, "Just lay it on me; I'm strong."

She again looked at the cards and pointed to the Queen of Spades. She said that this person was causing my problems. It wasn't anyone in my family. She was sure of that, but she was the one.

I started making bad jokes and tried to sway her from her statement, but I couldn't.

She picked the queen up, rubbed it and said again, "She's the one, she's an." She stopped, said a few zodiac signs but dismissed them. The person's sign, according to her, was not a true sign but rather part of two signs.

I asked her what she meant but she didn't acknowledge me and just kept on searching her mind and finally, she said, "February, the beginning of February." She said it with a great deal of satisfaction as if she had just solved a mathematical problem.

She reassembled the cards, reshuffled and spread them out before me and told me to pick five cards. She turned the cards over one at a time and there they were a pair of kings and the Queen of Spades. I was shocked. All the card tricks I had ever seen the person performing, the trick handled the cards. She started to reaffirm what she said before, but the other two cards that were turned over weren't picture cards and now for the life of me I can't remember what they were. She pointed to the kings and mumbled something I couldn't understand. "She," motioning toward the queen, "is in a state of confusion and the confusion and unhappiness is affecting you...as long as she..."

Before she could finish, I picked up all the cards and felt the sides of them to see if they were a marked deck. I realized that the cards had been spread out before me and I made my own selection. This was no card trick that I could detect but logically, I couldn't accept what she said. She kept talking on while I got up with the cards still in my hand. I put the cards down, asked what I owed her, paid her and left. While I was walking out the door she was asking me if I was all right and to call her again. I just kept walking. She almost yelled after me not to worry because everything was going to work out that I would solve whatever problem there was...

I got in the limo, and settled in for the ride. All the way home I felt embarrassed and vowed I would not relate what happened to anyone. I don't know why, except to say I could not deal with what I was feeling or more importantly, my ego was bruised because I could not explain it unless I used terms such as feelings, psychic, and psychiatrist. These words are just not in my vocabulary. I could not imagine myself seeing a psychic after seeing a Cardinal. I made a silent pray that God was busy that day that maybe he missed me going.

Russ sensed I was very uneasy and other than a few humorous remarks to get me to relax, as he put it, the drive home was uneventful and, thank God, quiet.

Once home, Russ volunteered to take the driver to where he had to go and as they left, Russ turned around and shouted after me. "The letter, don't forget the letter! I tell you, it's your salvation!"

Russ, from the first time I related to him my thoughts and feelings, such as they were, told me to make believe I was writing her a letter. The monsignor had in effect told me the same thing. I stood in my driveway for a moment.

I nodded and disappeared into the house. As the tail lights of his car disappeared down the street.

# Chapter Twelve

Once inside the house I pulled out the write up I was doing on Betsy...I began to reassess the events that happened and began to wonder what was really happening. I walked to the front room of the house, which I had made into an office/den. The room, although large, was cluttered with sofas, chairs, TV and desk. It was behind this desk that my best thoughts made their presence known.

Unfortunately, they weren't coming as fast as I would like. I tried to evaluate what was happening with Fields, but the bonus of the limo kept whirling around in my mind. I didn't believe that Fields had ever owned it or that it belonged to the company. After having that thought, I became annoyed at myself for even having it. "What's the difference?" I was shocked to hear my own voice.

"I'm going to call her!" Before I knew it, Fields was out of my thoughts and Betsy was dominating them. I imagined making the call and, for some unknown reason not being able to get through. "I'll leave a message for her to call me back!" I resolved. What happens if she calls back and tells me we'll have dinner...after dinner she calls me again only this time to tell me to get lost! What, what?

The mere thought of this exchange had me sweating profusely. My hands became sweaty and my whole demeanor changed. I sat down in the large recliner, leaned back and envisioned myself responding to the mythical phone call as though it had happened.

Her mythical call absolutely devastated me. I heard the words but unfortunately they didn't fully register until after she had hung up. I wasn't quite sure what she said, but the words you should get on with your life, stuck in my mind like a weight that was around my neck. I couldn't for the life of me understand how she could have said such a thing. The reality of the situation I was in came back into my mind as I got up from my chair, put on a jacket and went for a walk. While I was walking, I was trying to remember what else she said but "get on with your life" just crowded everything else out. How glib those words sounded as if they were rehearsed for a long time. Yet how could they have been...people just don't say stupid things...I just kept walking as if walking was somehow a cure for something. I came back home and sat in the big leather chair.

"She's right." I had said it aloud. "She's absolutely right." I repeated this to myself both silently and verbally. Here I am coming out of nowhere, disrupting another person's life -- a person who I have thought about for years even though I didn't know it. She in one speech tells me to get on with my life. She is callous, she didn't believe what I said, or she doesn't give a damn.

I felt as though she was with me as I said to myself, "In all the years that you have captivated my thoughts and in fact became part of them, I never in my wildest imagination imagined that you did not share what I felt. As I was reflecting upon my thoughts, I was trying to convince myself it's over. Your existence has been reduced to one imaginary dinner and handshake it's over. I am saying the word over and over in my mind as if somehow it's going to help me, but I don't think it is going to give me any solace. I must recognize this fact but no matter how I deal with it intellectually or emotionally I shall forever be drained of any emotion towards any human being. The mere fact that I know you're out there, or even after you're gone, my last conscious thought will be of you. As anyone goes through life he receives and expects certain setbacks and disappointments. Each time one must reach into the wellsprings of his being and resolve that he must go on. Even philosophically one tries to rationalize that each new experience will make him stronger. Somehow I am looking for such strength today but see none forthcoming. I am hoping that time will be the healer that makes me whole again but you have been a part of my being for so long, I don't think time is going to help me out."

All of a sudden I felt very old and very alone. The feeling of old doesn't really bother me too much since that's the scheme of things; I, as best as anyone, have adjusted to the fact of the passing of time. The hard part is fully recognizing that you will never be a part of my life. No matter how hard I try to accept this fact I just can't.

I continued my self-examination. "I try to fill the void that the absence of you has created but have not found the cure. The part that really hurts is that I don't think I want to. My thoughts of you I have always kept private, but now I can't do that anymore. I have a tremendous guilt inside of me that all these years, while being with another person to whom before God I professed my love, I find that the words spoken were a fraud and each day I perpetuate the myth I am being forced to live in my self-proclaimed and created purgatory. I just can't believe that you're not with me.

I keep asking myself how fair is it for me to keep living in a situation wherein I am lying and continuing to lie by my presence. I am having great difficulty in not admitting that the marriage I entered into was not a fraud. A fraud of the worst kind in that I took another human being, professed my love for her and now after one dinner and a handshake have difficulty in continuing a relationship that has been built on 32 years of deception. I have got to be the worst kind of person on earth. How do I justify, if not to anyone else except to myself, the position I find myself in. God, in his infinite wisdom, has decided to create a hell on earth and I guess I'm in it.

I have tried to convince myself that I should consider myself lucky, for some people I'm told, never have any such experience and go through life never feeling for anyone. But somehow, even convincing me of this thought doesn't help much. I'm strong, I guess so, like any other disappointment or sorrow that was dumped into someone's life, and I'll just have to go on. But that phase usually means to build upon the ashes that are left. Somehow I just don't feel that strong. How does one close his mind to something that has never been and yet been inside for the majority of his life? I know there must be a way.

By now, the leather chair had become too hot for me to sit in any longer. My clothes were drenched. I got up, went upstairs to take a shower, anything to stop this vise that I felt I was being squeezed in. After a fast shower, I stood in the bathroom. What would happen if she really did say, "Come to dinner"? What would I have done? I realized that I was now standing nude in the middle of the bathroom having a conversation with myself. I quickly dried myself and started to get dressed. I sat on the edge of the bed and again the thought of her came back. I imagined an entire scene of taking her to dinner. The problem was that after such a long time I find myself completely defenseless against you. The person who has been my constant mental companion has in one sense become a person I am beginning to fear.

The fear I find is one that has its roots in my own incompetence and not with her. Driving to pick her up I could see her so clearly all the way there. When she came to the door I was shocked because I couldn't see her as I had for so many years but rather as a living person, worn down by the years and by what had transpired to her in her life. I was afraid that she was going to disappear again. There she was on the other side of the storm door and I didn't know what to do or say. She opened the door and motioned me in because I was afraid to enter her townhouse or say anything. My throat was dry, my palms sweaty and I could actually feel my heart pounding in my chest. I always had thought when I read phrases describing scenes like that it was pure fiction. At my age I finally found out that those feelings do exist. I am trying to think back as to how long I was standing in the doorway and I truly don't know. The only thing I do remember was at the split second I saw her it was as though time stood still. Or worse yet, I didn't want it to move because I didn't know what I would do.

She saw me standing at the door and invited me in while she got her jacket. The next thing I knew I was helping her put her jacket on and trying not to touch her all at the same time. I finally had to calm myself before I had a stroke. She smiled and I started to breathe again. I was so mad at myself and yet I didn't know why. I don't remember saying anything as we walked out the door and I waited until she locked it. We walked to the car. I was so glad that I had brought the limo because there was just no way could I have driven. I kept fumbling with the door. Finally it opened and she got in. For the first time I remember saying something. "You have to slide over." I couldn't believe I said something so stupid, but realizing I did, I just kept quiet.

The drive to the restaurant was short and I am positive I said something but I don't know what. Thank God we got there and I could get away from her and get out of the car. That feeling of wanting to get away I find was not to get away but rather to be able to see her in a different light because until we were in the restaurant and seated next to each other was the first time I felt like a human being again.

She smiled and it was as though we were all by ourselves. I don't know what she was saying but I couldn't wait for the waiter to come over to take our order...first for the wine, and for dinner. We started to have a conversation and I started to feel more relaxed. The wine finally came and I swallowed two glasses full. I swear it felt like water, but it did calm me down.

The night just flew by and the first thing I heard was that there was no 'we.' My surprise must have shown, because the next thing I heard was she doesn't go out with married men. I felt a sudden surge of rage shoot through me. I kept my composure. I told her I was most definitely married and that there was most definitely a 'we'! She asked me why I had gone through such extraordinary efforts just to find her. I found that before I knew it there was someone inside of me talking to both of us. It was like sitting in a lecture hall listening as someone else related my life and feelings over the years. I still felt as though I was dreaming and I was sitting by myself.

I finally took a deep breath and took her hand. She was real. It was easy to tell that emotionally she had been drained. When she looked at me, the fire that I had remembered in her eyes was gone or if not gone, not shining as brightly. I felt that I was drained too, for all the hurt she had experienced. She had called out for help and I felt it but did nothing about it. It was these feelings of inadequacy that have been driving me nuts all these years and with greater intensity these past months, weeks and days. The cry for help had gone unanswered and she was left by herself.

She, in one step, left being a woman of the '50s and was thrown into the '90s, a strong independent person who had to fight all the fights of life herself. As she was talking, I kept thinking about similar situations that occurred in my own life, but I was there to handle them all. I should have been there to handle hers as well. I still don't know where I'm going with this relationship but am completely alive since she said she would help me come to peace with myself. I couldn't believe that she was willing to help me even after I had failed her so miserably.

The ride from the restaurant to her home flew. As I walked her to her door, I didn't know what I was to do and I was relieved when she extended her hand to mine and thanked me for a nice evening. When she touched me, my arm froze and my hand went limp. I left and went to the car. I was actually glad that I was leaving but I knew that I wanted to see her again, although I realized that I never saw her the first time. There I was sitting on the bed with one shoe on, holding the sock for my other foot.

Off in the distance a phone was ringing but it was too far away. I was completely spent, I lay down to sleep, half dressed, one sock on, one sock off, saying a silent prayer that sleep would not be replaced by anything else.

# Chapter Thirteen

The meetings of the "big six," as it was often called, were the six directors of the company whose job it was to handle special problems, was called to order by Mr. Fields tapping on the side of his cup. The same six men were present and the maid was told to leave. She quickly went into the kitchen and made sure the recorder was working. She called Tony and informed him as to the meeting.

The wall separating the two rooms was still open and Mr. Fields rechecked the room to make sure everyone was gone. He started. "Gentlemen, you all now have had an opportunity to reflect upon the events and personally seen and heard George. As far as I know, the only people who know what happened in any meaningful way are George and Henry, our self-created Frankenstein."

"What about that Smith lady?" one of the six asked. "Did our new friends from Italy, the Marinos, decide to expand their orchard?" Everyone laughed.

"Do they have room for two more trees?" one of the other men interjected and again everyone laughed except one.

"George isn't going to be too easy to plant. When he went there unannounced, they not only met with him immediately, they had a big party for him so that he would meet the rest of the 'dignitaries.'" Fields was about to say something but the man speaking just waved him off and got up and started encircling the table. He continued, "Our reports said they called him 'Mr. George.'"

"Mr. George from America," someone else interjected.

"I stand corrected," the speaker said. "When you," motioning to Fields, "assured us that after your meeting with George at that restaurant, that, and I quote, 'we will be done with him,' not only did it cost the ten thousand we were going to save, but half a finger as well." No one laughed or in any way broke the mental silence in the room. The speaker continued. "No, Mr. George from America is not the easy person you have tried to convince us that he is. Rather someone who has taken the best we have...and mastered them. Who is this girl he keeps thinking about? That may be the answer we're looking for. How reliable is this information Russ is providing us with? Can we trust Russ? And let's not forget George's ever present Tony...Can we meet him?"

The speaker by this time had completely encircled the table and sat down. "This question must first be answered or else decided if we are to ever find the man's...What's that Greek's name with the bad heel?" Everyone laughed.

"Fields, call your green bonnet in." The speaker continued. "You know the one who would have no trouble at all with Mr. George."

"Beret," one of the other men interjected, "Beret."

At the beginning of the meeting Fields had handed out a resume on the three people he had hired. Everyone took a moment to read it before summoning the first one to the room.

As his four and a half fingers grabbed the doorknob, he was reminded of the incident that made him be reminded every time he tried to perform the most basic of all maneuvers. As the man walked into the room, there was a nervous smile on the faces in his audience. He was 6'4" tall; he had been a tackle on the University of Alabama's football team. After college he was drafted by one of the professional teams. He opted to go into the Army and from there went into the Special Forces unit commonly known as the Green Berets. During the last exercise before graduating, he turned his knee. He thought nothing of it. That night a game of one-on-one basketball for beers brought him down. Three operations later he was out of the armed services and trying to get a job...any job. Mr. Fields recruited him after being screened from over a hundred candidates. Fields wanted to create his own inner-company police force, since many company executives were starting to be kidnapped or threatened while leaving the company traveling through foreign countries. The lists of uses for just an internal police force just continued on. Fields had convinced his board that three people were necessary, two men and one woman.

The other man hired had a background similar of armed services also, but insubordination was his downfall. After service he was brought to realize all too soon that he had to follow orders. His first assignment for Fields was to handle George in the restaurant. The experience scarred him for life and cost him partial sight in both eyes. His nose required two operations to get some sort of semblance to being normal. His decision not to stay in security business was made for him by his doctor, a decision he never questioned. While in the hospital, he would amuse himself and his visitors by saying, "It's a tough business when the other side can hit back."

Miss Smith was the third of the group. She was recruited in the 6th Street gym in Miami, long used by boxers from that area. Famed boxing trainers had seen her work out and set up a few bouts for her. Just local bouts since no nationwide promoter would touch her. She could challenge anybody in the gym that was in her weight class but, of course, everyone declined, each using the excuse, I can't hit a woman or I'll kill her.

One time one young boxer was taunted into the ring by Mr. Field's generous offer to pay him $1000 to get in the ring with Miss Smith. Fields had heard about Miss Smith from his people and went to the gym to see the beautiful dynamo. She knocked the challenger out in one minute and 26 seconds of the first round. Fields hired her right on the spot. Unfortunately, Miss Smith had now disappeared.

No one knew where she was and no one cared enough to find out. She was an orphan who would never stay in any orphanage or foster home. She had no one and no one wanted her.

From the three people that Fields had handpicked and touted for their physical abilities, only one remained and he was crippled not so much by the loss of part of his finger as the loss of the toughest kid on the block title.

He just stood in the center of the room while the members of the board looked at him. No one said a word. After what seemed to be an eternity, one of the men said in a voice so low that it was barely audible, "Could you excuse us, please?"

Nothing else was said until he left. The gentleman continued. "I will not trust him...Fields...I will not trust him. See if we can get Russ or Tony or this girl George has nightmares over. We have to find someone who's close to him that he wouldn't expect or suspect. I don't want him coming after me."

Fields was having difficulty breathing because of his anger. "I'll try," he said. "I'll try." The meeting was adjourned while Fields stormed out of the room.

"There's our problem," one of the men said.

"That's it," he said as he was motioning towards the door that Fields had left by.

"Where's George?" one of the men asked. Everyone who was seated at the table looked at each other and, finally, the silence was broken.

"He's home, I guess."

"Fields didn't invite him to the meeting."

"He's home."

"Shall I call him and ask him to meet with us?"

"No!"

The discussion between the men continued as they examined their options. On one issue, they were right. I had gone home after the meeting with Fields. The meeting was concluded and the remaining five went home. Once they left the room the maids came in to clean. One of them picked up the resumes to get them to me.

I was still at home in bed. I began to stir but remained in bed trying to think of a reason to get up. I laid back and, as though there was a switch in my head, I was daydreaming again. I envisioned myself seated at a table talking to someone that I could not quite see and began to relate my feelings to the imaginary person.

I began searching my thoughts the way one searches a house looking for something he's lost. The item I was searching for was the thing, event or some sort of trigger that made me recall a person after so many years. I retraced every route I took; every place I went and even everything I had said, or was said to me to try to find some logical explanation for my current thoughts. The only beginning I could remember was traveling north on the Hudson River...that's when I began remembering my old school days. There was no connection that I could figure out between the river and my school days.

The woman at the racetrack...she reminded me of someone. At that time I didn't know who. I didn't know then, but I know now! The boat ride and the track were two independent things, and although related to the case, weren't related to why I should be recalling events and people, or more precisely, a person some 50 years later! That poor woman at the track must have thought I was nuts...I am now beginning to agree with her. This case and my thoughts have nothing to do with each other. It's like writing two books simultaneously and trying to merge them together when there is no connection except for the fact they, for some unknown reason, happened during the same time of my life.

I said, "Being a direct person, I figured the best thing to do would be to locate you. In this way I feel I would put my mind at ease if I just knew where you are and what you are doing."

"I find that I have never really thought about what you have done, only your present circumstances. My ego makes me feel that whatever they are if you are unhappy about something I will be able to solve the problem. Don't think that I am being a blowhard; it is just what I feel, and I cannot explain it to myself. I guess I am not doing a very good job of explaining to anyone else. The only thing I must admit that stating my thoughts at least allows me to air my feelings to the only person who could possibly understand this burning sensation in me every time I think about you. I have tried to explain to others, but to no avail. They don't understand it either."

"Ever since we left high school you have always been in my mind, but I never quite understood it. Driving past your house at first was done as a matter of necessity because of where it was in relationship to where I live, you live, and my destinations."

"It started to become apparent to me that no matter where I was going, your house was on the way."

"At first, I just dismissed it as just plain stupidity, and later I just categorized it under idle thoughts; and I mean idle thoughts."

"After graduating school, I had a fleeting thought of calling you or somehow finding where you were, but I wasn't too proud of myself and therefore dismissed the idea as being too stupid. After all, what does one say to a 'thought'? But still, no matter where I was going or coming from, your house was en route!"

"One snowy morning while driving to work, I was in an accident on the corner where your house was. I was driving past, I took my eyes off the road for a moment, and someone ran into my car. I thought it was you or someone from your family."

"I remember sitting in my car half wishing that it wasn't because I didn't know what I would say or do, and at the same time, wishing it was. I didn't have anything to fear since it wasn't you or any relation. The first thing I remember, some guy standing outside my car yelling at me and firing questions at me as to what I was doing; what I was looking at, etc., etc. I really didn't hear him but rather found myself going through the motions of giving him the necessary paper work and realizing that I didn't get his. My insurance company took care of everything and I didn't have to deal with it. It took me a while to get used to the fact that I almost 'ran into' you and at the same time, feeling very disappointed that I didn't."

"At one point in my life, I had to leave the area so I bought a new Chevrolet, white convertible with turquoise interior. I took a trip around the country and Mexico. I worked odd jobs around the country, but after a while, decided to come home. By the time I came home I resolved that I would find you, but I didn't know why."

"When I returned, my lawyer called and asked me to meet with him. He wasn't only the family lawyer, but a close member of the family. At the meeting he told me I should consider returning to school and that afternoon, Farleigh Dickinson University was giving an entrance exam to the Rutherford campus. The next thing I knew, the President, Peter Samartino, was interviewing me. He admitted me in, even though I didn't have all of the requirements, but with a stern warning. 'I'll let you in, but it's up to you to stay in.'"

"That June, we had our five-year reunion. I couldn't wait. I had gone to the Poconos for the weekend, but drove back for the reunion. You weren't there or at least I didn't see you there. The rest of the night was a blur and the drive back to the Poconos was the longest in my life. I remember driving to the reunion, planning what I would say, and what I would do. I don't know why, but the thought never occurred to me as to what you would do or say. I guess I just assumed that there would be some common ground for us to meet on. I had everything planned and as I drove to the reunion, I kept going over our future in my mind."

"When I didn't see you, and no one seemed to give a damn

that you weren't there, I was devastated. I left and tried the rest of the night to forget how foolish I had been."

"The next six years passed like a blur. Between going to college during the day, and working at night right through the summer, I was a person possessed. I had by this time resolved that I was going to be a lawyer. I don't know why or when I reached this decision, but that was what I was going to do, and I did. My lawyer was very pleased and encouraged me to go for it. I graduated college with a degree in accounting and merchandising. I wound up with two majors because of a mistake in the scheduling by the school. The way things worked out, I was lucky, since the first interview I went on was for a job in fashion at Saks Fifth Avenue in New York."

"While attending college I had written a paper on merchandising in the field of high fashion. My teacher had sent the paper to his friend who worked for Saks, and I was invited to New York. I walked in, and the personnel director looked at me and told me straight out that there was no way I would I would ever get a job in fashion, no matter how good my paper was. He said my physical appearance would never be acceptable in the world of fashion. Need I say I was devastated? The very next day, I had an interview with a regional accounting firm."

"Much to my surprise, I was hired; the only non-Jewish person in the firm. This job allowed me to work days and go to school at night five nights a week. That left Saturday and Sunday to study. This schedule left me little time for anything else. On those nights I could go out. I would frequent the bars in the area where I thought you and I would go together."

"When I would meet someone we graduated with, I would inquire about you. When they responded that they didn't know anything about you, it would destroy me, but at the same time give me great relief because I was afraid that I wouldn't know what to say or do if I did meet you. Now I feel confident that I would have overcome whatever psychological hang-ups I might have, but I don't know."

"It was during this time that I met a girl who would later become my wife. My problems really began...How do I marry one person, and still not be able to forget another? I was so ashamed of myself, and my feelings, especially that by now it had been some years since I had seen you. I resolved that I would put you out of my mind before I could continue any relationship with another person. We had another reunion, but again you weren't there."

"The years again became a mist since I was married, raising my family of three girls, and changing careers. During this period of my life, my thoughts of you became more sporadic and separated by longer periods of time."

"From the accounting firm, I became the sect treasurer for a private company and after seven years, I opened my own law office. That was the scariest time of my life...a wife, two girls, and one on the way. Just plain hard work became the order of the day."

"The thought of you disappeared. Another reunion, and no you. I just accepted my own shortcomings by not having the sense to seek you out and went about the business of just living and providing for my family."

"We had a forty-year reunion. At the time of the reunion I was going through some sort of depression, or maybe it was some kind of realization that I had been married to a lovely woman who had given me thirty years of devotion and three wonderful children, who in turn gave me two granddaughters that I adore."

"I just couldn't bring myself to go to the reunion. I guess I was afraid you wouldn't be there, which I would have taken as a personal rejection. Even more frightening would be the possibility that you could have been there, and in all honesty I didn't know what I would do."

"Since, the thought of you has permeated my very being. Each day that goes by seems to intensify my need to see you. I still don't know why, but I must at least try."

"I went to our grammar school, and looked up the names of everyone in the class and told everyone that I wanted to have a fifty-year reunion."

"Next, I went to our high school, to review the records which didn't add anything to what I already knew."

"Now I am going to follow up every lead until I find you, and maybe this stupid obsession of mine will cease."

"I recalled what the monsignor had said about writing everything down so I wrote a letter last night until I fell asleep, and here it is morning and nothing has changed. I am starting to wonder if this letter writing is all that it is cracked up to be. I decided to continue the therapy this morning."

"I have tried to envision where you are or what you are, and I just keep hitting a blank wall. I just keep getting this urge that I must somehow find you."

"Although I had asked Russ to help and about everyone else I knew educated in finding people, I just couldn't sit still. I knew somehow I had to get involved. My friends in the various governmental agencies responded to my calls with the usual 'don't worry' and 'we're on it,' which at first satisfied me, now fell on deaf ears. My own stubbornness just kept on me like a stern headmaster in schools or yore."

"I decided to make up a list of people we graduated with from grammar school, and look in different neighboring town's phone directories. My first attempt proved successful in that I did, in fact, locate a fellow student in a neighboring town. What became more eerie was the fact that I knew his wife as well as and both of them asked who else I had contacted, but of all the students, they asked specifically if I had found you."

"The question had an unnerving effect on me. I kept a friendly conversation going, but the content of it just escaped me. I must have sounded somewhat coherent since we chatted away about many different things, but the reason I had called was not advanced at all. With the usual promise to get together sometime, the call ended. The only positive effect it had was to give me faith in what and the people who ran them. I reached out for them to see where that would get me."

"The yearbook from school was on file at the high school. Yellowed by age, with pages that had become brittle with age, the school graciously loaned it to me to continue my research. The book had the students listed who had graduated from high school and it worked out that of the thirty from grammar school, only seventeen had gone to high school in town. The book also listed their last known address. I carefully closed the book, so as not to destroy any pages, and returned it to the school with my thanks."

"My idea was to draft a letter and send it to our classmates, and asked them to contact me with any information they might have on any other student. I thought at first, that the idea was truly inspired the results from it were less than satisfying. In fact, it turned out to be a waste of time. People just don't respond to the written word. I made a second mailing of the request, but this time I included my phone number and that at last, brought in a few responses. With these new leads, I again started a telephone campaign, and was again busily hearing about everything and everyone, but not about you."

"I was able to contact the gentleman who had handled the first high school reunion after a great deal of difficulty. He had moved away, but one of his relatives still lived in town, and through his relative I was able to make contact. Again, the phone conversations were pleasant, but they did not advance my knowledge about you one iota. The one point that he did emphasize was that if I wanted to find the ladies, I would probably have to check the Town Hall for marriage licenses to get their new names."

"I knew that since when I was practicing law for a period of time. I only practiced divorce law and was well schooled in name changes, marriage licenses, etc. Defending bad guys or advising people on how to 'save taxes' is bad enough, but to break up a marriage and see two people turn into animals was more than I could take, so I had to stop handling divorces. That was probably the darkest of my professional career."

"I went to Town Hall to continue my quest and can only hope that what I am doing is the right thing to do. I must confess, I still feel uneasy about this but I know I will feel worse if I don't continue."

"Since I started the 'reunion' I seem to be tenser rather than relaxing. With every call, letter, etc., I start to have mixed emotions about the response I will get. When I ask specifically about you I can actually feel myself holding my breath and I have to tell you, it seems like an eternity before I get a response."

"The search has given me a tremendous education as to the absolute arrogance of public employees...and I found out that it isn't limited to them. The minute I tell someone what I want, I get a standard response on how hard it is going to be and how busy they are. However, after I tell them that I am a lawyer, and the information I'm requesting is not going to put our nation in jeopardy, they comply."

"I have tried to rationalize what is happening to me over and over in my mind, but I guess I'm just not that smart. I called a friend of mine who is a priest and an overall nice guy, and explained my problem to him. His first response was that I should write down how I felt. When I replied that I already did that, he suggested that I continue to write, hence this extension. However, all was not lost since he told me that if I found out where you were baptized, they would know if you had gotten married. When you marry, the church that marries you must notify the church where you were baptized."

"It really works. I started canvassing local Catholic churches and found where you were baptized. When the lady from the church called me back with the information in less than ten minutes, I was really shocked. I was informed you were married in a nearby town. I went to there and obtained a copy of the marriage license. On it, was listed the witnesses of which one was a classmate. Her brother is still a doctor in town and is wife is the receptionist. When I called her to get her married name, I received the complete history of the entire family. I wanted to shut the receptionist up but I couldn't without being rude. Anyway, it took her awhile before she finally gave me the information I wanted, so I excused myself, and hung up."

"I called your witness and again had to wade through the chatter before I could bring your name into the conversation. At that point in time I really didn't want to know the answer. I just sat looking at the phone as if I were waiting for someone to jump out at me. I actually put my hand over the mouthpiece; of course, I realized that her voice was coming from the other end of the phone. She told me that your marriage didn't work out and that you were down in South Jersey. I was actually elated to hear that you were divorced. I couldn't believe I was actually glad to hear about your misery. For the moment, I was so glad and yet mad at myself to think that I was enjoying what I was hearing. I can only say that I am really sorry to hear that things didn't work out for you since I told you before at one time I only did divorce work. I have lived through more divorces than most people have seen with all too much vividness what divorce can do to a person. Unfortunately, I can only apologize in this letter."

"I was told that her sister, was still in touch with you and that I should contact her. I stopped myself from calling. I was actually trying to examine my own motivation for continuing what I was doing. My priest friend kept asking me what I was going to do once I found you, and all I could say was that I felt as though I was in a dark room and out of this blackness I sensed your voice and presence. I felt ashamed because I did."

"I called the only real lead I had, but of course, I had to wait to hear from her."

"When she finally returned my call, I was not home but she was kind enough to leave the information I wanted on my answering machine. It is surprising and embarrassing to explain how a phone number in and of itself could have an effect that paralyzes. To hear a number left on the machine was chilling, to write it down and read it was an even greater shock. I could not do anything but look at it for what seemed an eternity. I put the note pad aside and decided not to do anything. I knew I had to call and I knew when I heard your voice; I'd know it was you. The forty-four years since I spoke to you would just disappear. For one of the few times in my life, words just escaped me. The next thing I knew I was babbling about how I found you. That wasn't really me talking, I was saying the words but my mind was racing in too many directions. I was stunned by the fact that there I was talking about your divorce. I really don't know how I could be so callous. I guess I messed up a scene I had rehearsed for a long time. Somehow, I just can't believe that what I said so badly is going to have an impact on what happens next. It can't, I won't allow it. After contacting you I called up and canceled all other avenues I pursued in trying to locate you. I told them, 'It's over' and to stop. Everyone, including Russ, complied. He, of course, had already found you but was debating with himself whether or not to tell me.

Unfortunately, I am going to have to continue with the facade of a reunion unless I can figure out how to get out of it gracefully. Somehow, you are going to have to help me. I don't know how, or whether or not you want to. Up to this point, all the decisions were easy since I could make them all without regard to logic, feelings, outcomes, results, and all of the other crippling effects that I can conjure up. Unfortunately, the battle of some sort is still in me and I don't know what to do and the only one who is going to be able to help me is you...I think! I have never known me to be so undecided about anything. I could write a defense concerning a defendant's life a lot easier than I am able to write this. At sixty-one, I am starting to realize that there is more to being alive than family, working, and surviving."

"I thought of all the questions I should have asked but hadn't. All the things I wanted to say but didn't. I don't know why I didn't get in the car and drive to see you, or else not called you and just come to see you. I guess I'll have to wait until I hear from you before I do anything. Somehow that just doesn't sit right with me. After researching your life in order to find you, you know that I'm not going to stop researching until I find out what you are doing every day. I just keep getting this sick feeling that I have been somehow responsible for any misery that you have suffered in your life. But if nothing else, maybe by so doing I will be able to deal with myself and settle my own mind."

"The other problem I have is that when I will hear you speak, I will be completely disarmed. I have made a good living because I could always keep my balance with any judge, jury, and other attorney and yet I am afraid to speak to you over the phone and I come apart at the seams. I am beginning to dread the thought of seeing you or even being in your presence, yet I feel ashamed that I am even thinking this."

The letter writing finally helped, I fell back to sleep. Letter in hand, pen in hand, but at last sleep came to me. I would doze off but again woke with a start. I tore the letter up and went to sit in my big, reclining, leather chair. The therapy didn't work. I tried to sleep but kept thinking.

"There's no doubt in my mind if I should ever try to see you. If I do, to what extent? I still haven't been able to come to grips with this. I guess I can only hope I don't make a fool of myself. I've learned that if you're willing to work and think hard enough, there is always an answer for every problem. I've got a sick feeling that, that isn't going to be the case."

My phone kept ringing. The answering machine came on and at the end of the message; Russ's voice came booming over. "This is the third time I called in an hour. I know you're there...Get up. I'm on my way." I heard the message, but I didn't want to react to it. I was hoping that I could disappear or move to another planet...I just didn't want to face Russ...I'll die...that's the answer, I'll just die...maybe if I just lie here, he won't know the difference and he'll tell everyone I died...for a while I drifted off, but was reawakened by the reality that nothing changes unless I change it...the problem being what to change and does everyone involved want a change! That was my last conscience thought as I fell asleep again.

# Chapter Fourteen

There was a pounding on the door. It was Russ. I opened the door and Russ, first looking around to make sure no one was home, turned and with an accusing finger shouted, "They're going to kill you! Do you know Henry's dead...Dead, damn it...No one knows where Miss Smith is...The two goons have been retired...You're the only one left...they're going to kill you!"

I was now awake, not from the content of the speech but from the volume of it. "Why me?"

Before I could say anything else, Russ continued. "You're the only one left who knows what happened...The only one...Everyone else is dead...Dead, man, dead." As he spoke, his volume increased with every word.

"Russ, it doesn't make sense that they would want to continue this thing. They have everything they want. Why would they jeopardize what they have? It doesn't make sense. All they have to do is sit back and make their profits again. Why would they want to come after me? And anyhow, how do you know so much? And don't give me that spy bullshit again." By now I was awake and alert and I started to walk around the room in between the sofas, chairs and desks.

"Stand still," Russ said. "You're making me dizzy."

"They don't trust Fields, that's why, but they like Tony and me...they want us to work for them and guess what our first job will be? You, damn it, you."

"Russ, you and Tony aren't killers. Anyway, I'm busy today, tomorrow...tomorrow."

"Jesus Christ!" Russ shouted. "Where the hell are you? Are you alive? See what I mean, you're not here. You're somewhere in space. You're thinking of her. Wait a week; you promised me you'll wait a week, we'll go see her...Please listen to what I'm saying."

I sat in the chair with my head bowed and nodded my approval.

"Did you write her a letter, yet?" Russ added. "That's it, write her a letter. You're a great one for writing. Write her a letter. You don't have to mail it, just write it. By writing, you'll be able to organize your thoughts. Anyway, that's what you always tell everybody else!" Russ had now reverted back to his old self, snapping his fingers and doing a little dance as he said the last phrase and started toward the door.

The phone rang.

"Okay," I said. "I'll call you tonight about ten. I have to write a letter first." Without waiting for a reply, I picked up the phone... listened...and hung up. "It was Fields," I said. "He wanted to set another meeting."

Russ smiled and started to leave again but turned and said, "Don't forget one week, that's seven days, one hundred sixty - eight hours, ten thousand and eighty minutes and six hundred and four thousand eight hundred seconds from right now." He slammed the door as he left as he was chuckling to himself.

I got up and finished getting dressed. I had determined to go to my boat. The boat was the answer. The bouncing on the water and the smell of the water would clear my head. The boat was about an hour and a half drive away. When I arrived at the boat I did all the perfunctory things necessary to launch it, and when the motor started right up, I felt I had made the right decision. An hour or two on the water, he will end this Fields thing and this Betsy thing and...and...and.

As I was sailing along, the little compartment on the center console of the boat popped open. I went to close it but a small packet was in the way. I removed it and opened it. There were three pills. At first I couldn't believe it. I remembered they were the ones that I had received in Saratoga; the ones I was to give to Miss Smith. There they were. I closed the compartment, closed the packet back up, put it in my top pocket and vowed to enjoy the rest of the day on Barnegat Bay.

Unfortunately, drifting off into my dream world no longer was a voluntary act. I imagined myself sitting at my desk; pen in hand, thoughts ready and starting.

I'm writing this letter or memo to myself because I just don't know what else to do or how to express my feelings or more importantly to whom. I have transcended to somewhere between running up and down the street to sitting quietly in a corner contemplating the future. This feeling surely must be hell. To be blown around by the winds of indecision is to say the least, no fun.

When I think of you, I feel so completely alive. I feel as though I was just born but when I reached for a piece of paper on my desk and couldn't read it without my glasses, I was quickly and most certainly brought back to reality.

I don't know if we will ever meet or if we do, what will come of it but I do know that the mere anticipation of meeting you and the reality of talking to you has given me an inner peace that I have not had for many years. I am at quiet with myself.

How easy it is to hide from reality if one likes to read. Not being with you created a void that I didn't know the cause of. The void was there, but not the reason. The book is a shell into which one could crawl into like a little room when pangs of loneliness began to bite. I know the feeling. The only difference is that the more I read, the better grades I got, and the withdrawal from the reality of the circumstances earned me more degrees. I used to marvel at people who, even to this day congratulate me on what they perceive as a monumental, intellectual, achievement, from junk man to lawyer in one leap. Someday I'm going to tell the truth that I didn't do anything but hide from what my life had become; a not too pleasant existence. The ironic part of it was that on one bright day there was someone giving me a degree for not facing reality. Of course at the time I received the degree, I reacted in the acceptable manner by putting on a wishful look and explaining how hard it was. That was plain bullshit. Now as I reflect on it, I can't believe that I was so weak while everyone else thought I was so strong.

The other day I lunched with my friend the priest and he was telling me how proud of me he was. He was actually elated by my "success." I was sitting there thinking of you and how weak I was not to just drive down and see you. He was jabbering away and I wanted to stuff a napkin in his mouth. I felt horrible and there's someone who has known me for over 40 years describing someone I didn't even know…me. He kept talking away, and finally I just couldn't keep quiet any longer and started to tell him about you. He finally shut up. At first I really don't think he believed me but little by little, he began to believe (the only reason I'm saying this is that he stopped interrupting me). He became more nervous than me. All he kept saying is, "What's going to happen?" I couldn't believe what he was saying and I had to have him repeat it. He thought it was because I didn't hear him, but I heard him…I just didn't understand him. There he was, asking me the very question that I was asking him. He started to tell me about someone he remembered from…Before he could finish I just shut him off. He had the brilliant idea that what I should do is write down what I was experiencing. I became annoyed at him or I guess at myself; at him for assuming I didn't really think of "writing my woes," and at myself for "writing." It's the flip side of reading.

One thing has become crystal clear to me. Today is today. Yesterday isn't doing anything for me except to remind me that it's past. Tomorrow is going to be what I make of it…but no more hiding.

I told myself not to expect "too much" because you're 61. It was like someone shot me. I don't know why I said that. As I am sitting here waiting for the time to pass before I can see you, it's like waiting for a jury to come in, only this time I'm not the lawyer, but the party.

I'm going to stop this dreaming now, not because it helped me, but because I don't want to hide behind it. I'm not smart enough to know what I should do; nor can I predict what you will want to do. To quote an "old cliché," I have to feel that "together" we'll find an answer. The more I thought about what I was experiencing, the more it bothered me since I felt as though I was assuming an awful lot and I was getting involved in an area, my feelings, that up until now I never really dealt with. The question open to me was what to do.

The quickness of the arrival of the dock finally brought me back to earth. It was as though the boat had stopped and the dock was coming for me. I docked safely, and after securing the boat, made my way to the phone. This thing with Fields had to end...Betsy is another story.

I grabbed the phone and dialed Russ's number. "Russ," I said without waiting for a reply, "Get Tony. We're going to end this tonight. Russ, Russ, are you there?" I became annoyed when I realized that I was talking to the answering machine. I slammed the phone down, double-checked that the pills were still in my pocket and drove home.

# Chapter Fifteen

When I arrived home the first thing I did was call Fields to set up a meeting. "I want them all there."

"Who?" was his reply?

"The bastards on the other side of the mirrored wall...all five of them plus you make six...all six...And you tell your goons to stay away...No more playing...away...We are going to resolve our differences or settle them but it's going to be over...over, God damn it, over!"

Fields acknowledged he understood and that he would try.

"Try nothing. Whoever isn't there, I'll get...So help me Christ, and I'll get!" With that I hung up the phone. I realized I hadn't said where. I called back immediately. Fields answered again.

"Rio Limo!" I shouted. "We will meet at Rio Limo. You remember where it all started? Be there at eight with the other five!" I again hung up and walked away. I had to end this thing but I was having difficulty in identifying just what this "thing" was. A mistake was made. There was never any doubt that a mistake was made, only how much the company wanted to pay for that mistake. Jurors and judges around the country, if left to normal channels, would assess the valuation of the error. In these types of lawsuits the jury assesses damages but the judge can reduce it if he thinks it's too much or increase it if he feels it is not enough. Either side can appeal, of course, but that still leaves the amount to be paid in a group of old men's hands; men who couldn't make it as attorneys so they hid behind the robes of justice; men, who out of the robes, wouldn't even be allowed in the same room as the big six. The respect that a judge commands is not based upon personal achievements but rather upon the position he holds, a position granted by some politicians, not by the market place. The base question to be asked is: should those people who were closest to the problem be allowed to rule their destiny or should those people isolated as much as possible from the real world be entrusted with it?

Weighing the different arguments and counter arguments was not only time consuming, but also very tiring. I tried to sleep. "I'd better rest up for tonight," I said to myself. No dreams, no nightmares, in fact, no thought processes at all, that's what sleep is all about. With this strange determination, I dozed off.

The phone was ringing with such a zesty tone that I jumped up fully alert. "George!" I shouted into the phone.

"Russ," came back the response. "Eight, tonight?" Russ was, as usual, right up on things.

"Russ, where do you get your information?" I asked.

"From the Fields, oops, I mean, the horse's mouth," Russ replied with his usual joking tone. "I won't come with you but I'll be around. Tony will be with me so if you need help, just press the belt and we'll be there...Well, Tony will be there, I'll be leading the cheers: Rickety Rick, Rickety Rack, come on Tony, break their back."

"Eight o'clock at Rio Limo," I responded.

"George, you're such a traditionalist. Back to where it all started. I love it." With this, Russ hung up and I began to get dressed. I made sure I put on the belt. I always wore this particular belt. It was leather with a brass buckle, two brass loops for the belt to go through and a brass tip on the end of the belt, very fashionable and noteworthy. In the brass tip was a transmitter and if I needed help, I would press it and Tony or whomever else would receive a signal and know to come bursting in with guns blazing. I was in big trouble.

I called the driver and told him to be at my house at 7 p.m. I wanted to be at the restaurant early. The driver, Brian, was a young man who had a natural talent for driving and keeping his mouth shut. He wasn't big by any yardstick, but could handle the car as good as anyone and better than most. "Brian," I told him, "just stay in the car...always...if I tell you to go, hit the gas and get me out of the area as soon as possible. Don't think about it. Just go. When your transmitter goes off from my belt, I want you by the doorway you dropped me off at but stay in the car with the motor running ready to get away...you understand?"

"Yes," came back the weaker reply.

Brian was on time and I was ready. I walked to the car, opened the door to get in. As I entered the car, I tripped and instinctively my hand shot out to grab something to steady myself. Instead, I grabbed the telephone that was in the car. I ripped it right off the side. Behind it, a microphone popped out. At first, I thought it was part of the phone, but on closer examination, I saw it was a microphone used as a bugging device. The car was bugged, but by whom?

Whoever it was heard every word that was said in the car since I had received it as a gift from dear Mr. Fields. The other possibility was that the cops did it, but why? Either way I had to find out, but once I found out, so what? What sort of reprisal could I take against either one of them? What good would it do? I sat there for a moment assessing what had happened, but came to the realization that regardless of who did it wasn't going to change anything I was doing, so why waste the time and effort it would take. I pulled the device out of the car and sat back for the ride to the big meeting. Brian got me there quickly and was fortunate to find a place to park right in front.

I walked in and was immediately greeted by the owner who brought me into the back room. It had been redone. The walls were all repainted with new pictures and the ceiling had been redone. It now looked like the evening sky. The doorways were still in the same place but all with new doors.

The exit door looked as though the safety lock on the inside was fixed so that the door could be opened from the outside. I went right over to it and fixed it so it could only be opened from the inside. The owner was shocked at my actions. I just turned to face him. "I hope you're not going to be stupid, are you?" The owner shook his head. The tables and chairs all looked new or at least refinished and the tablecloths and napkins were a lavender color. The place really looked nice but not like the rest of the restaurants in the area. This room had been transformed from a Portuguese restaurant's dining room to the dining room one would find in a corporate office.

"You did all right the last time I was here." I said. The owner again smiled. "I want a table set for seven with an ice bucket for wine set next to my chair." As I pointed to one of the chairs I said, "I don't want anyone around us and two waiters by us. They are to take our order, leave, bring our order, leave and not come back until I call them. Understand?" The owner nodded his head. "Keep everyone else away from us, okay?" Again the owner nodded. I went into the bathroom to make sure the doors were as before and came back into the dining room to supervise the setting of the table. All the silverware, glasses and dishes looked brand new. This guy did all right for himself last time, no wonder there were no charges brought or anything else heard of the incident. The floor had been scraped and refinished. There wasn't any trace of what had occurred there before. Even the salt and peppershakers looked brand new. The new lighting system could be dimmed so that the room took on a whole different view. The waiter was going to light the candles on the table as they stood there so majestically in their new holders.

"No candles," I said and they were quickly taken away. The doors to the kitchen had been replaced but still were swing doors. At last I felt comfortable and at ease so I sat down and awaited the "big six."

At exactly eight p.m. all six came in. I didn't know who the other five were since I had never seen them, but had felt their presence. What if I was being set up and Fields just brought five other men with him? It's too late. Now they're here. Judging from the way the men were dressed and the jewelry they were wearing, I felt comfortable that these men were the ones I wanted. Fields started to make the introductions but I waived him off. "I've ordered an array of dishes and hopefully there will be something you like. The waiters are here for your dinner and drink orders, so I suggest you order now so that we can get on with this meeting." Everyone seated themselves around the table and gave their orders to the waiters. Everything was done with great dispatch so that when they were done, everyone sat down and looked at me to begin.

Fields started to talk and the other gentlemen motioned for him to sit down. "We want to hear from George," one said. I knew I had the right group.

"Gentlemen," I started. "I was hired to do a job and I think I have accomplished everything you wanted me to." I looked around but could not make eye contact with anyone. "I am now confronted with the decision of what to do with all of you since I am told by 'the Street' that you people want to get rid of me." All of the men sat straight up on their chairs. They took quick glances at each other but were reluctant to say anything. "If I am wrong in anything, please tell me but one of two things is going to happen tonight. I'm leaving here knowing I am in complete compatibility with all of you or none of you are leaving. There can be no other way. I'm not going through life worrying about any of you. We're all in our fourth quarter of our lives and I want to enjoy mine." The men looked at each other not fully realizing what they had just heard.

Fields was the first to speak. "Are you really threatening all of us?" he asked with a smile.

"You're first," I said while offering everyone one of the appetizers. "You have to have been some kind of sick individual to give me a gift of a limo and bug it." The other men stared at Fields. Fields turned red.

He was the one, all right, I thought to myself. One of the other men sat up in the chair and tapped his dish with his fork.

"We have listened to you so that we can better evaluate just what our relationship should be. From what I've heard here, you want to leave happy and confident that we aren't coming after you or we're dead."

I started to speak, but the man just continued, "We have no argument with you, but you must appreciate we will not be intimidated by you either. We did not bug your car but since Mr. Fields belongs to our group, we will have to deal with him...That's us, not you...It is true that we are very pleased with your results and I for one was very impressed by the method used but we cannot, nor will we condone threats. Now, what I suggest is this. You, I am assuming, have no desire to continue to work for us."

I nodded.

"The only question is whether or not we can convince you that we are not interested in pursuing you any further?"

Again I nodded.

"Well, for reasons that should be obvious to you, we are not interested in making any new enemies since we have enough already...We are interested in continuing our lives without having to look over our shoulders...We at least can agree that we will part company, if not friends at least, with confidence that this is the last time we will see each other...I, speaking for everyone, can say that it has been a pleasure dealing with you and to the extent possible, accept my word as chairman of the group that this thing ends right now!"

At this point, Fields winced in his seat. I was listening but more importantly I heard the rattle at the exit door as though someone was trying to get in. I nodded to the speaker my approval. I got up and waved to the waiter to bring me a tray of glasses. From it I selected seven glasses. I opened a bottle of Portuguese Green Wine and poured seven half glasses of wine. I turned to put the bottle back and took three pills out from my pocket and dropped them in three glasses. At long last all the pills were accounted for.

Up to now, everyone had assumed that Miss Smith had destroyed the three pills from Saratoga as she was instructed to. Miss Smith always carried out her instructions. The exit door rattled again. I picked up the tray and each man took a glass. "Gentlemen, I propose a toast to a job well done and well paid for. Let us leave each secure in the knowledge that we will never see each other or speak each other's name."

Everyone drank. The exit door was now rattling violently. I put the glass down and walked into the men's room. I pressed the belt as the door into the bar opened. Tony and Russ jumped to their feet. As they got the signal they looked up and there I was motioning to the front door. Brian, upon receiving the signal, started the car, put it in gear and was ready to leave. As Tony, Russ and I got to the front door, four men came running in almost knocking Russ over since he was first to reach the door. As soon as the men passed, Russ, Tony and I went outside and got into the car. Brian pulled away and took Russ and Tony to their car and me home.

The next morning the headlines read: "Three directors of a large pharmaceutical company resigned each stating health reasons."

Russ was at the front door of my house ringing the bell and pounding on the door. I opened it and Russ asked, "Why three? Why only three?"

I motioned for him to sit down, poured him a cup of coffee, sat down and looked at him. "Russ, when we stated we didn't want the company to be ruined, we achieved that...I didn't want them to bother me any more so I think the three remaining ones will tell the three new ones to keep their part of the bargain and at the same time keep a certain continuity going in the company."

"How did you get Fields?" Russ asked.

"That, I didn't do. He had an equal chance." I laughed to myself because really it was the truth.

"Let's forget about all of this," Russ said with a beaming face. "Let's go to Atlantic City for the day. I'll call the driver. Go get dressed or whatever."

I, like a well-behaved child, got dressed and both Russ and I waited for the driver to come to take us to the wondrous city.

The rest of the day was spent in idle chatter, a show in one of the lounges, gambling and on to another casino for the same routine all over again. Dinnertime came and both of us had dinner in one of the gourmet restaurants with an ample serving of wine.

"Here," Russ said. "Have another glass, this way you'll sleep all the way home."

After dinner, we met the driver at the designated time and place and settled back for the ride home.

# Chapter Sixteen

As the car sped away into the night, the darkness engulfed it as if it were wrapped in some black paper. I sat there staring out the window into nothing but the blackness of the night. It was as though all the lights had gone out in the world and all the stars left the sky. I felt myself sinking into a depressed hypnotic trance. Who am I kidding? I want to see her even if only a vision. How can I profess to want to forget her...when, at every moment, I want her? I can't just call her, but why not? What would I do with her if we did meet? Where would we go? What would we do? I can see the headlines now: 61-year-old grandmother and 61-year old grandfather die while in their love nest. The biggest problem with time is it takes its toll silently and without much fanfare. I should find out what her financial situation is. What the hell? She was only a teacher...with two children...two, and a divorce. I wonder if her husband ever gave her child support. She probably had to struggle to make ends meet. That's what I'll do. I'll get her financial records and see how I can help her. If she has a mortgage, I'll pay it, what the hell. That Trump guy did it, accept it will be hard to follow her around until I get a flat. I don't think she could change the tire even if she wanted to. I should have let Russ take her picture...He did; I was just too stupid to look at it...I wonder if he still has them...I must really be sick...Here I am just totally disregarding her feelings, privacy and solitude but, hell, that's the nature of things...If everyone respected everyone else's privacy and all that other bullshit, Eve would have had to eat that apple herself...No, every law no matter how just on its face still has got to be applied with some degree of common sense...She can only say "no" if she finds out and when she does find out and she's mad, how can she stay mad...No...That's what to do...I should go see her...The hell with Russ's theories and fears. He didn't know her...She wouldn't be rude to me. The most she'll say is it's nice of you to call but good-bye...What will I do? I can't be in any worse shape than I am now...We're both mature adults...A lot of water has passed under both our bridges and recognizing this, I guess we can develop a relationship...As to what that relationship is will have to be worked out between us, but that isn't so bad...She's been married but left because of adultery...That had to hurt...But what caused it? Maybe she isn't the person I envisioned all these years. Nobody strays from the nest by themselves...All those divorce cases I handled, the wives always held themselves out as being the ideal mate and loving wife with an overabundance of love and understanding...I never could understand if that were all true, why would any man stray from someone like that to be with the type of woman that the ex-wife would describe to me...Maybe Russ is right. I'd better rethink this thing through...No...There's no way that she could be anything but great...She'll know what to do and she'll know what I should do...All these other people I go to see aren't any help. She at least will have a better insight and guide me at least since my handling of this matter isn't working too well...One thing for sure I'm going to have to face up to her and these constant nagging thoughts...The ride back from Atlantic City was going to be a peaceful one. I made that promise to myself. The car was picking up speed and for the first time the sound of the tires became more acute. I tried to dismiss it from my mind but the rhythmic beat continued.

I stared out the window trying to think away the sound as the air within the car increased in intensity. I shook my head as though it would do some good. It worked. I kept trying to think of other things but the blackness on the outside of the car invaded the interior. Somehow I felt that if I could keep the three elements apart in my mind I could beat this loneliness monster at its own game. As long as I felt I was in control the fear was avoided. I fought a brave battle but like all battles there is a winner and a loser. I suddenly felt myself losing this one. For I realized, without all three she was not present either. I was winning. The more I thought about winning the more I realized I was losing. My internal strife made me fall victim to the air, sound and blackness. I was in its grip again. I kept thinking that fighting a dragon was what I should be thinking about not trying to avoid a feeling that encompassed and held me so tight that all other thoughts were kept out. I began to wonder if fighting a dragon was as bad as it was made out to be. At least I felt I would be able to see it. This monster was inside of me and I could not get to it. I could not bring myself to realize that the monster was caused by not being with her. That realization was the worse scare of all.

Russ's yelling and shaking me brought me back to reality. "My God, George, are you alive?" Russ screamed at me. "What the hell is in that window? No, don't tell me it's that bitch again...Listen, you're not going to be any good to yourself or anybody else until you deal with whatever the hell it is...Listen, I sent her flowers and enclosed a nice card. I told her that you would call tomorrow...I was speaking for you, of course. I wrote I didn't want to startle you by just calling out of the blue after all these years so I thought the was the most appropriate way of initially contacting you...I hope you don't mind? I signed your name. I didn't sign it. I had the florist do it. The florist was so nice. She just thought it was wonderful that I was doing this. She thought I was you. The way that florist was carrying on, she sounded like she was crying. I gave them your credit card numbers, of course, and I was going to include a box of chocolates. You know what a romantic at heart I..."

"You did what?" I asked in disbelief. "What the hell did you do? I ought to choke you right here!" I thought for a moment. "But, thanks. You're right. Going on the way I'm going is ridiculous...Russ, I owe you. Now all I need is the courage to do it...I will...tomorrow!" My words came out in staccato fashion.

The driver had reached the house, and Russ and I got out. The ride back from Atlantic City is never as long as getting there. The car was parked and the driver left. Russ bid me farewell. As he was leaving, he half turned. "We'll have to go on a double date. You know the old worrier, the skinny old school teacher, the man about town and the florist." He continued to laugh and dance all the way to his car. I stood in the driveway convincing myself that I was awake...No dream, but awake...Russ had done what I should have done months ago.

The night dragged on as well as the next day. I wasn't sure what time I should call. The morning paper, again carried the story on the three directors of a large drug firm had resigned and I felt a certain amount of satisfaction as I read the story. I started to jot down what I was going to say but after several drafts just crumbled up the paper and threw it away.

"It's a phone call, just a phone call," I said. I could not concentrate on anything; I could wait no longer; I picked up the phone. Russ had supplied me with the numbers and my hand slightly trembling started to punch the necessary numbers.

I sat at my desk and started to think of all the reasons why I shouldn't call. Over 40 years and I never spoke to her seems to be the best reason of all. I could not think of one reason to call her. She had lived her life without me and now after all this time I would be interfering with it. I tried to think of what I would say and as I sat at my desk I could not think of anything after I said, "Hello." I tried to envision what she would look like hearing a voice coming over the phone that she hadn't heard for over 40 years. What if she laughs at me and just hangs up? She would never do that. I don't know what she will say or do, but rude she won't be. I thought of driving out to the school where she taught and just wait for her to come out of school and just walk up to her and say, "Hi, I'm George, remember me?"

I sat back and envisioned how ridiculous I'd feel if she said, "No." I might scare the hell out of her but at least I would be doing something. Sitting at the desk staring down at the phone was becoming a slow torture. I looked at my hand that somehow had been detached from the rest of me and saw it trembling. I jumped to the back of the chair stiffened up in it and became very annoyed at the way I was behaving. I got up and walked around the room. Calling her became an obsession with me or at least I tried to tell myself it had become one. I clinched my fist as though I was about to enter an arena to fight some mythical beast and went back to my chair, sat down and ordered my hand to stop shaking. With an iron willed determination I picked up the phone and in one motion dialed the numbers. Before the first ring I made a silent pray that she wouldn't be home and I swore I would just forget the entire incident. I would just eradicate from my mind.

The first ring of the phone startled me but not as much as the voice that came over it as her voice came from the receiver as she said, "Hello." I swallowed, for my throat had become so dry I couldn't speak. "Hello," the voice said again.

I knew it was her. All I could say was, "Is this Betsy?"

The inevitable long silent hesitation followed, the kind of silence that is ear splitting.

"Yes," she finally said. "Who is this?"

"Would you mind saying that again?" That response was the only thing I could say as my mind went blank and my throat went dry.

She made a slight laughing sound and over 40 years evaporated. I felt as though I was back in school with her. No time had passed from the last time I had heard her voice, again a short-long silence.

"Who is this?" she asked again.

I gather within me whatever was necessary for me to speak

and responded, "I sure hope you're sitting down, this is George."

I could hear her gasp, as again there was a light laughing sound and she said my name, "George." She said it as though she was shocked to hear my name and yet she remembered me as though we were together only the day before. "How did you ever find me? I haven't seen or heard from you in how many years?"

She kept talking, but what she was saying was incomprehensible. I was still getting over the shock of talking to her and hearing her voice. I became annoyed with myself, for I was no grade school kid but rather a hard crusted professional. No matter how many times I told myself that I still felt like a school child trying to ask a classmate for a date. I tried to listen to what she was saying, for by now she was becoming insistent on finding out how I found her.

I quickly responded, "I don't know. I can find out the specific steps involved if you really want me to. I just told my associates to find you and when they told me they did I was just happy to get your phone number so I didn't ask anything else. If it's that important to you I'll find out."

I was mad at myself for not creating a better answer than that while at the same time being happy that I was able to say something. My normal breathing pattern came back and I was glad that I could breathe again. My self-confidence began to build as I started asking general questions as to her well-being and before I knew it I said, "Let's go to dinner and I'll answer all and any of your questions. I called to see if we could go out. Dinner would be nice but whatever you say will be alright, I guess." I could not believe I said that. I was becoming annoyed at myself for sounding like an idiot. I quickly started to calculate how long it was taking her to answer since I felt that the longer she took the better off I was.

"Well," she started again. "I have to…"

Before she could finish I interrupted her with, "Look, I understand that you were not expecting this call. I mean, it has been a long time. I'll call you back on Monday and by that time you'll make up your mind and check your schedule of events. Decide what you want to do and we'll get together. There are a lot of nice places by you, so pick the one you want."

The silence again became unbearable, for I didn't know what I would do if she said "no." I sat at my desk staring at the phone that had now become my mortal enemy.

Finally she responded, "Alright, call me then."

My heart jumped right out of my chest. I must have said "goodbye" or at least I think I did. I got up from the desk, for all of a sudden my chair had become very uncomfortable.

I walked around my room mumbling, "This used to be easier." I still felt a great amount of pride for finally calling her. The only reason that I could figure out for feeling as I did was my conquering of my fear of rejection. "What would I have said if she said 'no'?" I dismissed that possibility and resolved that the days were going to pass slowly until I called her again.

The day finally came and I called for the car early. The driver came and he could feel that there was something happening. He knew that tonight would be different. The driver backed the car out of the driveway not knowing where he was going but most trips start on the parkway. The silence in the car was too stifling.

"Where are we going?" the driver finally asked.

I mumbled something, but quickly repeated it. "We're going back many years. Take the turnpike south."

The driver was befuddled by the first statement but said nothing as he headed the car south towards the turnpike. I sat in the back of the limo trying to think of something witty to say when at last I met Betsy. No words that went through my mind seemed to satisfy me. I started to have a silent conversation with myself as I tried to understand why I was even going.

Would I recognize her? Would she recognize me? I had changed my clothes three times and still felt uncomfortable in them. It was a lot of years since I saw her and now as that time was dwindling down to an hour I, for the first time, started to question why I was going. The thought of seeing her that night in Italy made me shudder again as I still had a hard time convincing myself she wasn't there at all and all I saw was an illusion, a dream, a ghost. I was still not sure what I should call what I saw but, I was only sure that I saw her. Since that time my very being was directed towards finding her. And when at last I did, I felt completely inadequate and foolish for going to see her. She must think me a fool. She had to, for as the miles that we were apart dwindled I was feeling more foolish.

The exit appeared out of nowhere and the driver slowed as they came to the tollbooth. By now I had given the driver the directions I had received from her when we spoke on the phone. I was ashamed to tell her that I had already driven to her house but lost my nerve when it came time to ring the bell.

I thought back to that evening when I was just going to walk up to her door and say "hello." I then thought of walking up to her as she walked to her car as she was leaving her school where she taught. I had gone to the school but lost my nerve when I got to her classroom door and decided to leave. On the way out of the school someone had challenged me as to why I was in the school but I just pretended not to hear and kept walking. I was glad when the custodian who spoke to me decided not to pursue the questioning. I was in no mood to talk to anyone at that moment since I didn't know myself why I went to the school.

I smiled to myself as I realized I knew why I went and lost my nerve at the last moment. In any event I was glad that the custodian just let me be.

It was after the school incident that I resolved to call her first. Calling her would be the most impersonal way of contacting her. It would be easier to accept the fact that she didn't want to be bothered with me if all I had to do was hang up a phone. That wasn't the case; here I was going to see her. The last few miles seem to take forever as each turn in the road seems to add hours to the trip. Finally the last turn was made and the driver pulled into the area in front of her two-story townhouse.

"It's over there," the driver said as he pointed to a doorway that had a light shining next to it. The outside light on the townhouses was the only one that was lit. Should I turn around and pull up to the door?" I sat for a moment looking at the door and the feeling that I had felt that night in Italy seem to over whelm me again. My hand trembled as I reached for the door handle. The driver was waiting patiently for me to give him further instructions and was becoming impatient.

He asked again, "Should I turn around and come up to the front door?" His impatience showed in his voice.

"No, I'll get out her," I replied. "You go turn around and come back." I got out of the car as I hoped the brisk night air would have some effect on me. The air was just air and of no help as I waited for the driver to pull the car out of the way so I could walk across the driveway and go to the lamp that, by itself, seemed to light up the entire area. I walked over to the doorway and started to have second thoughts of what I was doing there. I tried to envision what she would look like but all I could see was the picture of her standing on the water and in my room in Italy. With a trembling hand I pressed the doorbell.

I could hear the chime ring and a voice from inside say, "Come in." I walked through the door with every fiber in my body trembling. I stopped for a second as I became aware of my uneasiness and became annoyed with myself as to why I was feeling the way I was. I walked through the doorway and back 50 years. Betsy was standing on the far side of the room. The air in the room disappeared as I stared at her. I was still not sure whether or not she was standing in front of me or if she were another vision. She had not changed from the person on the beach.

My tongue became so thick in my mouth that all I could get out was a weak, "Hello."

I heard her inviting me...I saw me dressing...I saw me being driven to her house. I envisioned driving up to her door, getting out of the car and walking to it. I was greeted with a warm inviting smile and invited into the town house. The rooms were just as I imagined, neatly decorated in a symmetric fashion. The colors were all blended together so that nothing specific caught your eye and yet everything belonged in the harmony with everything else. On one of the end tables, there was a magnificent arrangement of flowers I couldn't help but think that Russ certainly has class. I can't wait to get that bill. Betsy was wearing a long flowing white dress that buttoned all the way down the front. The dress was not buttoned down as far as I thought it should be but I was ashamed at myself for even thinking like that. She motioned for me to sit down on the sofa.

I complied and stared into space waiting to catch sight of her again. I was trying to say something but nothing came out. I heard some rustling noise but didn't think anything of it. I wasn't able to move anyway. It was as though my entire body went limp and yet was keenly alive at the same time. She had poured two glasses of wine. She offered one to me and took the other and sat down on the other side of the room in a straight back chair, the kind with fancy covering on with brass tacks all around it. I don't know whether or not I was happy about the seating arrangements but felt that under the circumstances it was best. She was saying something and I was trying to look attentive while at the same time trying to drink the damn wine without spilling it. All this while, I was trying to breathe. I sat there thinking this is ridiculous...What am I afraid of? Who is this bitch anyway? I could feel myself gaining confidence, but I

175

didn't know what for.

"What have you been doing with yourself?" she asked. Before I could respond, she continued. "I understand you're an attorney and an accountant, but really, what do you do? You're an entrepreneur? Is that true? Now you promised that you were going to answer any and all my questions!" She said the last phrase as a teacher lecturing her class. I put the damn wine glass down when I finally realized she had put a coaster on the coffee table for me. I pushed the whole table away a little bit so I didn't feel so confined.

"Where should I start?" I managed to get out. "I've done everything not because I wanted to but I find that I get bored or else somebody offers me more money for doing something and off I go! I have been compared to a modern day mercenary." I caught myself. I didn't know this woman from Adam. She sits in that chair like a headmaster, a nice friendly headmaster, but a headmaster all the same. "I've done what I had to do to support myself and my family. I've been luckier than most or I've been willing to work harder...I don't know which is needed to succeed, hard work or luck or nerve. I guess you have to have some ability too, so I tell everyone that I had all four elements, luck, nerve, ability and the willingness to work hard in the right proportions at precisely the right time."

By now I had completely gotten up and encircled the room three or four times. "Am I making you uneasy?" she asked.

"No, it's just me. I can't sit still for more than five minutes at a time...I should have warned you about that." Half running, I went back to my spot on the couch and sat. "You're the one I want to hear about," I said. "I have to find out if there is any correlation between the things I've been feeling and the events in your life."

"What do you want me to tell you? I graduated high school. I went to college...I worked for a couple of school systems...I got married; had two children; got divorced and continued to work. I can retire next year and I'm going to."

"What happens if you retire now?" I asked.

She looked at me as though I came from Mars. "How will I pay my bills? I have to live, you know," she said.

"Well, all I'm saying is, it's a number. You take what you make less the taxes, etcetera, which will give you your net cash income. Have you computed that? If you stop now, will it affect your pension or health benefits and if it wouldn't quit!"

"Well, just how do you suppose I pay my bills?" she snapped back.

"What the hell, I look like I only got an olive branch and a mule." The words came out with such force that she was taken back as though she was hit. "I'm sorry," I said. "My god, I'm sorry...it's just that I have a personal hurt or something I feel personally responsible for your problems, anxieties, or whatever or I guess I just feel I should do something or more exactly, I want to do something. Please don't be mad at me. I didn't mean to offend or insult you...Oh, shit...Can we talk about something else?"

She looked like she was still stunned by not only the meaning of the words but the volume at which they were said. "Are you joking?" She finally managed to get out.

"Do I look like I'm kidding?" I asked, but in a much softer tone that was barely audible. "Decide what you want to do and let me know and I'll set it up!"

"George, I'll not be a kept woman. I'll..." She kept the flow of words up but by now, I was just caught up in my own emotion.

"Look," I said. "I'm not trying to belittle you in any way...You've got to believe that. We're sixty-one, not sixteen. A lot of people our age are dead. They spend their golden years walking in circles. I don't want that to happen to you. We can't have children together, but other than that, there's no reason why we can't enjoy everything else there is in life...Have you been to Italy? You must have been since that's where I saw you."

"I've never been there," she said.

"Go on one of those tours or allow me to take you...I mean, we'll go on the same tour if you want and I'll plan the whole tour...You'll see Rome, The Vatican, the place where I saw you..." I suddenly realized that Betsy was not being impressed by my offer or if she was, she was doing a good job of hiding it. "Or," I said in a singsong way. "No strings, just take the extra year off...What the hell can it cost? I'll defend one of those skinheads. My fee, if and when I collect, should be more than enough to cover it." By now I was more relaxed and smiling. I got up and walked to Betsy, took her hand in mine. "I'm very serious. I'm not kidding, nor will I expect anything...ever. Please allow me this one favor. I'm doing it for me, not you..." My voice trailed off and she turned and went back to the couch and sat down. I drained my glass and just sat.

Betsy got up, picked up my glass and refilled it. "George," she said. "You sound like a person who has a very nice family...and I know you do...I've done some checking also...You love them very much...Consider yourself very fortunate and leave it at that."

"What you say is true, Betsy," I responded. "And I'll do all that, but don't ask me to feel fortunate...I can't do that...I don't know why...No one seems to be able to help me...But what I feel inside is tearing me apart."

"I am sorry. The experience I went through would never allow me to go out with another woman's husband. I just could not be part of something like that."

The words came at me in a barrage. I did not want to hear them for I knew she was right but mad because she was. I was still dazed as I made my way to the door. By now my eyes were full of tears that I could not control. I felt ashamed and hurt as I made my way out the door.

The silence that filled the room not only muffled all sound but seemed to consume all the air as well. On the table next to the door was a box of tissues. I took some out to wipe my eyes so I could see...I could not breathe...I opened the door and the driver, seeing the door opening, started the car and drove to the door. Betsy came over to me and went to kiss me but I just pushed her aside and went directly to the car. I stumbled in and the driver shut the door behind me. I sat quietly as the driver put the limo in gear and pulled away. Betsy stood in the door and watched the car until the taillights were no longer visible. She went inside and closed the door. Throughout this entire scene, there was not one word spoken.

She pushed the coffee table back to where it was, fixed the pillows on the couch and went to bed. The drive home was done in complete silence. I was half asleep and not quite awake. "George, George, you're home." The driver announced.

I went inside like a robot and lay down and tried to sleep in my big easy chair fully clothed. The constant buzz from the phone brought me back to reality. I wasn't sure what had happened. I realized I never had pressed the last numbers. I hung up the phone trying to figure if it was a dream or a nightmare.

# Chapter Seventeen

In the days that followed, it was a strange feeling to wake up in the morning and spend the first few minutes analyzing how I slept. It must be an experience limited to the old. To compound things, I had to evaluate how Betsy slept which in retrospect, really is stupid. For years I had functioned reasonably well as an attorney and accountant. Each of those professions demands a certain type of regimentation in one's thinking. Now I find myself in some never-never-land that is illogical and yet may very well have an enormous impact on my life, or better stated, on what was left to my life. The equation becomes more impossible when every morning I am having breakfast with my wife and enjoying it.

The words of the Monsignor gave me some peace because even he said, "There is an answer—there always is." But the faith and reliance I placed on them were quickly diminishing. With clenched teeth, I would pick up my pen, get a new pad and set about the task of outlining a solution. I guess the real problem was that I was the only one who knew there was a problem. This fact alone, being the only one in a love triangle, gave me the greatest difficulty.

On one side I did want to retire, which was quickly taking on the definition of finding something to do which was different from what I was doing before. To this end everyone tries to be helpful. The suggestions are never ending as to the quantity but are all the same as to quality. It seems to boil down to golf, volunteer work at a hospital or church, and travel. I am convinced that there is nothing else. It is as though I was standing at the edge of the Big Black Hole and there is a sign at the bottom with the word "retired" on it. All these things existed before and somehow they were acceptable and to some extent inevitable. Now when I look at them they seem like insurmountable obstacles. I guess I have to face the fact it is not what you do but rather the people you're doing it with.

My wife, it never seems to amaze me how she can spend hour after hour moving around the house constantly busy. A trip to the store is prepared for and enjoyed as much as a trip to some exotic island. Any suggestion to doing "something" is met with an unending list of things that "must be done" and the complete exhaustion that much activity would create. None of these activities or answers had taken on a new meaning. I began to realize that she hadn't changed, it was me, or more correctly, the way I was beginning to perceive things. It was as though we were on the same plane in space but it was heading in two directions at the same time and yet keeping us together.

Betsy. She didn't know I existed, was never a part of my life other than in my daydreams or nightmares, never expressed a desire to become part of it, labeled the other woman while being totally innocent and not wanting to be the other woman.

I tried to explain the feelings inside of me to myself having a perfectly sound conversation; however the only person present was me. When I realized what I was doing that shocked me back to the ever-present reality.

After going through the usual morning's tasks of just getting up and accepting the fact that very little had changed from the day before, I would without even realizing it, begin thinking of how she slept and how her day began. The longer I thought about it really had nothing to do with the intensity. It was as though time was somewhere else and only affected me in the sense that I knew it was there, ever present and constantly moving. However, it acted only as a guard rail would, not interfere with the flow of thoughts but yet as a constant reminder that time exists and would be constantly restricting my movements. It was this thought, the fact that I may run out of time, that began to become a dominant factor. I guess as much as anyone, I wish there was some way of freezing time so that each person could reevaluate what they had done and plan what they want to happen but when trying to "wait a minute" today becomes yesterday, and tomorrow becomes today and yesterday gets stored somewhere in your mind not as it actually happened but rather how one wants to remember it happening.

The last conversation or event, or I guess the last anything, begins to take on a meaning that is more acceptable rather than what was actually said or done. I finally sat down and began to write a letter.

It began:

Dear Betsy,

I want to thank you for allowing me to know you. It has certainly been a great help to me. I don't know if you believe what is in this book, but it is the truth.

However, the reason for this letter besides thanking you is to tell you about a book I am writing. It is the first novel I'm trying. The story is about a retired advisor. While working on an assignment, he begins to envision a girl he knew in school. His health starts to fail which causes him to lose his nerve. He decides to "get out" and tenders his resignation. There is a big retirement party given but, of course, the true meaning cannot be told so it is called a testimonial and he is given a humanitarian award.

In the course of his medical treatment, he is referred to the Joslin Center for Diabetes. His treatment is in the hands of a young female doctor. From the time he sees her it heightens in his mind a constant nagging memory of a girl he went to school with and over the years could never entirely forget. The memories or fantasies plagued him and would increase and decrease in intensity, but always were present.

The intensity of which he remembers her increases to

the point where it starts to encompass his very being. In desperation he starts out to find her.

Not knowing too much about her and all he did know was from over 45-years-ago, the normal channels one follows seemed closed to him. While reading the paper one day, he sees an ad for names of people who had attended a certain school. Using a 50-year reunion as a cover story, he begins his search for her.

While searching for her, he begins to recall his past thoughts and visions of her and tries to align them with events in her life. Not understanding what is going on in his own mind he reaches out for help from other people.

They story line develops until he finally finds her and they meet for the first time after 45 years. They have dinner. After dinner they part and the woman makes it known in no uncertain terms that there never was a relationship nor does she want one.

The story ends.

After the letter was written, I proofread it three or four times and promptly tore it up in a thousand pieces. It's over...the end.

I was determined to get on with my life except I remembered that she has always been a part of my life, in different forms and intensities, but constantly present. No more. Done. Finished!

Once you go to the Saratoga area, the hotels and resorts in the area send you a reminder of the racing seasons and suggest that you reserve early. The travel section of the newspaper ran an article on the upcoming season at Saratoga and related events.

I read the articles along with the other articles and one advertisement described places to go around the world. All of the items seem to blend together and after reading the rest of the paper, which takes awhile, I dozed off.

The next day, being Monday, began like all other nondescript days. About noon I was thinking about where to go for lunch when one of my sisters walked into the house. I was startled by her presence. Before she could say anything, I invited her to lunch and quickly dragged her out of the house into her car. We had lunch in a local restaurant/bar and idly discussed the pressing problems of the world. We had to eat quickly since she wanted to go to the mall and of course I accompanied her. We went to the mall on Route 4 in Bergen County somewhere that I had never been to; parked the car and started walking around through the many shops, unconsciously or by rote I was reviewing the wares offered for sale and half listened to her incessant chatter.

There was the hat, the exact hat. It was off white with a floppy brim and a flower in the middle. I stopped dead in my tracks and stared at it. I was back at Saratoga; standing by the windows not quite hearing the names and the odds on each horse. I could just about hear my name being called or better put, I could hear the word "George" being called and somehow figured it was me.

My sister came over. "What the hell's wrong with you? Are you all right? Come on, let's go." She fired these questions and commands at me and started to become annoyed that I didn't respond immediately. "What's wrong with you?" She looked at me and quickly started giving me reasons why I shouldn't buy the hat from "that" store. "They're too expensive," she said, "Come on, we'll find it in another store cheaper." No matter how I objected, I found myself being hurried through store after store but could not find a duplicate of the hat I saw that day. Trying to convince someone like my sister that she can't buy something cheaper is an impossible task. No matter what amount of logic I used, she was determined. Consequently I didn't buy the hat that day. On the way home she started to question me about why I want "that" hat. The questions increased in both intensity and in number. I was trying to block out the incident out of my mind but found that to be impossibility also. We finally got home. I got out knowing that she was annoyed both for not finding a "cheaper hat" and more annoyed because I left her many questions unanswered.

I became very annoyed at myself because the very thing I didn't want to remember or, better put, was ordered not to remember and "get on with my life" had revisited me. I went back, paid full price and bought the hat, flower and all.

That night I would call her. I didn't know what to expect but convinced myself "she wouldn't be rude." Before I called, I went over in my mind exactly what I would say; how I would phrase everything, where I would pause, where I emphasize and when I would end. I laid out the call the same way I would an opening statement to a jury. I even started to rehearse it to myself but that was interrupted by my own ego. "I don't need a rehearsal," I resolved to myself. I pictured myself dialing the number.

The phone rang...She answered...I went limp. Her voice acted like a sedative and pep pill both at the same time. I said something and the next thing I knew this other person other than me was asking if she had a white hat with a floppy brim with a flower on it. I suddenly realized it was me talking. I sounded like some alien from outer space. Gone was the brilliant opening laid out like some music composition but in its place was the fumbling speech that I could not bring myself to realize that I was talking. I guess she recognized the fact that I was having difficulty organizing my thoughts so she graciously allowed me to ramble on about the different activities that accompany the racing season in the Saratoga area but at the end of my speech and her description of the straw hat she did own, the word "no" came through loud and clear. Not that it was said in a harsh tone but somehow the word "no" has harshness unique to itself and no matter how it is disguised, it still comes out "no," even in a dream.

I would try to get into the "normal" routines one is expected to do. I just became more annoyed at myself when I realized and recalled all the effort exerted and the energy spent trying to forget all about her was monumental...but ineffective. The exercise really frustrated him. The only problem was, the harder I tried the more frustrated I became.

I had to attend a business meeting where certain proposals for different projects were being presented. The idea being that if an investment opportunity seemed attractive to one or more participants, he would take the whole deal or a percentage of it and when 100 percent was taken, that deal was closed and the next one would be offered. The information you would be listening to was fundamentally financially presented in a rather detailed fashion that requires the listener to be completely focused on the speaker. During the presentation everyone was given a large yellow pad and pen for taking notes as well as a calculator. Since the topic concerned money, keeping everyone's attention was pretty easy.

There I sat, yellow pad and pen in hand, listening, even leaning forward in the chair not to miss anything.

The researcher had learned that Betsy's father had just died and her mother had moved in with her. Simple arithmetic, put the mother's age in the 80s and the fact that Betsy had divorced her husband led me to the conclusion that her mother never really had a son-in-law or at least never had a "good" one.

I made a notation to send her mother flowers for Mother's Day.

The speakers were still going on about how good this deal was over that one and how this one required no follow-up and would self-liquidate and how this was a better rate of return, etc., etc., etc.

I read the only note I had made during the entire meeting. Send flowers for Mother's Day. I thought, "If I do, that bitch will have a fit and I'll have to listen to a speech that I should not send gifts." The only problem was that I wasn't thinking it. I had said it out loud. Everyone had heard me and sat in silence and just stared at me. A stupid grin came over my face and I could feel my face getting red. Everyone could sense I was embarrassed and politely changed the topic.

I didn't hear another thing that was said. I don't even remember writing the note and felt really ridiculous that I now could not get her out of my mind but the infatuation was spreading to her family.

At the same time I remembered that I knew nothing about her children and grandchildren. I immediately thought of starting a campaign to find out about them but resolved that I shouldn't. As I dismissed the whole incident I did it with the fear or full anticipation that I shall be revisited or at least stand a good chance of being visited by the rest of the family. As each one of them makes themselves known I will first have to rationalize my way through it; seek a remedy resolutely try to put the whole incident and participants out of my mind, a task I am fearful that is beyond my capabilities.

# Chapter Eighteen

I began each day with a silent prayer that today would be the day I would be done with these recurring thoughts about someone I had yet to meet. I started to withdraw in a semi-retired state of mind and forgetfulness started to take the place of a keen, perceptive mind.

My aloofness started to show even though I spent my best efforts to hide it...but very quickly, I stopped trying to hide behind some self-made macho image which no one ever saw and I was never any good at portraying. I found myself thinking longer and harder about what could have been rather than being thankful for what is. At every moment I found myself writing letters or just wishing. It was though the amassing of these writings that this book became a reality. My friend and associate, Russ, would chide me about my wishfulness, but never dwell on it. Russ marched to a beat of a different drummer...his own exclusive drummer.

The discussions of Betsy diminished with Russ advocating their elimination altogether. I would generally comply...and any time I continued to indulge in my fantasy would I do so on my own...usually in the sanctity of my own home while sitting at my desk. I continued the practice of writing letters...mostly to myself...once they were admired, I would promptly tear them up. It was during one of these "dreamy" times that while drifting into some place...foreign to all...even me; I started to realize that writing ones thoughts down just doesn't work. Once recognizing that fact, I couldn't think of an acceptable alternative as ridiculous as I felt for doing an absolutely wasteful act I started again.

I sat down at my desk, really just reviewing the day's events, or better stated, reflecting over the situation, as it now existed. I couldn't help but realize that those things, which were inside me, never came out and feelings that are dormant in someone just stay there. Unless somehow or someway one can access them, they will always just stay there and fester. This feeling of helplessness just bothered me but after a while resolved that that is the way of life. Because one person feels one way does not mean that the whole world is going to agree with him. It is a strange sensation when, for the first time, you realize it. To try to attempt to solidify my thoughts, if for no other reason, in a really vague hope that I could rationalize them or deal with them in a better way than I was doing at the moment. I decided to write another letter. Not that all the notes, memos or letters I had written did any good, but I still hadn't come up with an alternative. Exactly who it was going to be addressed to, I wasn't quite sure but I felt that if I could put down in words that which was bothering me somehow looking at it on a piece of paper would make everything all right. Of course in reviewing it, I recognized the fact that it was really very foolish. But sometimes very down to earth, conservative people who pride themselves on always viewing in charge of their emotions of a situation do foolish things. So with paper in hand, neatly spread out before me, the pen being readied as one would ready a sword to do its work.

I sat down and asked myself, "Now who am I sending this to and what am I going to say?" The sound of my own voice startled me.

After some time I started, "Dear"…and somehow I just couldn't write her name. For some reason, nothing would come out. I sat there for a long time trying to collect my thoughts, which really was bothering me because that was something I never had too much trouble with…coming up with something to say…But here I was looking at the piece of paper with "Dear" written on it, tore it up, got another piece of paper, and started off again; "Dear" and this time left a blank. The only difference being from the first attempt was this time I left it blank purposely. I started:

This letter is meant to be a lover letter... I guess, but if not that... a collection of my thoughts. The word love itself started to bother me because rationally, how could I possibly love anything and certainly someone I never knew.

I tore the paper up, but this time with determination. I took out the third piece of paper. Now I was determined it's going to be a letter. A letter that's going to express my feelings and someday I'll mail it. So with pen in hand, paper before me, I was straight up in the chair and started. "Dear" and again a blank and again done purposely.

I have tried to set forth...I am going to try to set forth all those things, which I guess I should have said or I guess I should have done. But, unfortunately, there's a big clock someplace and that clock just ticks and no matter what we say and no matter what we do, it keeps ticking. Now, as I get closer to the end, I'm starting to find that maybe I had missed something in my life that I should have reached out for. It is like an old saying I once heard that goes, "I have now enjoyed some degree of success, some degree of happiness and in some circles, and I've been considered where I have climbed the ladder of success. But unfortunately, at this stage of my life, I'm getting to feel it's up against the wrong building." Not that I can complain, but somehow there is a void in me, which I've placed there myself, and because I have done that, it hurts all the more. I have tried to rationalize in my mind that because one person had a feeling toward another person, does not mean that that feeling is reciprocated. And that I guess I can live with because I've lived with it already. But the part I don't understand or I cannot accept is that I didn't even try. To attempt something and be turned away at least leaves you with something inside you that says, "I've tried." But never to try and never to reach out for something that you wanted, leaves a void and it is that void which creates the problem or creates the hurt more than a problem. Over the years, I have fantasized every different conceptual relationship I could possibly have for another human being. There has never been a day when the memory or the thought of, not memory, the thought of, being with you has been with me never. Unfortunately I am probably the most faithful, far admirer that anyone could ever have. As I review my thoughts, I say, maybe the thing I was fantasizing about just wasn't what I thought it would be. No matter how many times I try rationalizing my thought, namely because I think a person is a certain way. If I ever lived with or got to know you, you might have turned out to be an entirely different person than the one I've imagined. But even this thought does not deter me from the fact maybe, could be, and would be just doesn't suffice with more active words of "been there and done it." How someone could go through life in the fashion that they are stumbling along without really knowing why they're stumbling? Now it becomes rather confusing, as I am older and trying to reflect upon that which I did. The only true wealth I think anyone winds up with is the wealth that's gained by knowing other people, and if not by other people, than another person. Anything less than that falls short and the difference being that to fall short one just falls into an abyss that truly has no bottom. As I sit now and try to continue putting down my thoughts, they all seem to be getting jumbled up because it's being written from a unilateral position, namely, I'm the only one talking or writing in this case.

At this point I put the pen down and looked at the paper before me with the scribbling on it and just shook my head because when I re-read it, it just didn't make sense. The letter didn't seem to start anywhere. It didn't seem to go anywhere. It just seemed like a group of words set down in some confused order that if someone else were to read it, they would truly have difficulty. I put the letter aside and sat back in my chair. There was a knocking at the door...I opened it and looking at my chauffeur, I realized that Russ was coming over because we were supposed to be going to dinner. I put the pen down, gave the chauffeur the keys for the car and went upstairs to get ready for my dinner engagement but somehow the task of doing that was not strong enough to put that letter out of my mind. After I got dressed and was ready, absent my tie, I came back down and went to my desk. There was the letter still sitting on the desk but now beaming like a beacon at me...not for its literary worth, but rather as written proof that I didn't know what I was doing. I sat down again and picked up the pen and started to write again.

I continued with:

"As I continue to write this letter, it is becoming more difficult for me to say that which I want to say. My inability to do this creates a tremendous amount of frustration...A frustration in the fact that there's something in me that I want to say but can't...Add that to the frustration that there's something in me that wants me to do something and I'm afraid to do it. It is very true that just being able to think things through sometimes gives you an answer. Of course, I don't believe it and sitting here writing this letter, certainly isn't helping me. The confused state that I'm in is just going to worsen the way I feel – not towards you, of course, but towards myself. As my self-esteem starts to hit rock bottom, I have now got to recognize one very simple fact, namely time is taking its toll and what could have been, can't be now more. There's no way of rewinding the clock...and I'm certainly finding that out. As I finish this letter, if that's what it's to be, the only thing I can say in justification of it is that there's no happy ending...Therefore, it must be a true story."

I signed it, "George." I put the letter on the side of my desk, the pages still in plain view and I got up and put my tie on. I heard banging on the door again...it was Russ.

I opened the door to let Russ in. "Here, sit down. I just got to put my tie on and we'll go," I said as I headed for the closest mirror.

Russ, of course being Russ, said, "Man, you don't have to put on no tie on. Look at me; I just put on a snappy jacket. Like this jacket?" And he spun around and went into his little dance. "This is where it's at. A white shirt and tie, you'll look like a dinosaur. Go upstairs and get changed. I want you in the limelight. I want you right up-to-date. I want you at the state of art. You know, on the edge of the sword. You're still back in the...I don't know where the hell you are. But go get...come on."

I stood there..."What the hell is it with you? I'm just going to put a tie on...we're going to go out to eat and you don't even like the shirt."

Russ turned and said, "You know, I guess you're right. It's not the fact of the shirt, it's you... I don't know why but I walked through the door and I felt like I was walking into never-never land. What the hell have you been doing? Let's get going...you go get ready but throw that shirt away."

I got up and dutifully started walking up the steps and said, "All right, go ahead make yourself a drink. I'll be right down."

Russ, walking over to the desk, stopped, turned and yelled out to George: "What drink? You don't ever serve anything but water...you want me to have water? Not even a soda... but water. You really are a sport!"

I stopped walking and responded. "Sit down and watch television."

Russ was standing on the side of the room; he looked around and saw the letter. Russ being Russ picked the letter up and started to browse through it and suddenly he realized what he was reading. Again, it didn't make any sense and read like a bunch of words someone would scribble down without any rhyme nor reason, but because he had gone through there many months with me, Russ realized what I was writing. He read over the letter at first very quickly, just skimming it. He found himself sitting down and reading it. He looked up and all of a sudden he felt very guilty. Something that he felt was just a whim or some stupid feeling. He never realized the fact that these feelings affected his friend so deeply. When Russ got to the last phrase, "It had to be a true story because it doesn't have a happy ending." Russ was dumbfounded. He could not even make a joke out of it. For Russ, that was an impossible situation. Russ was sitting in the chair feeling tremendously guilty on how he treated my feelings and thoughts and acts in such a glib fashion. Something that the thought was incomprehensible to him was there on a piece of paper. Poorly written, or greatly written, depending upon how you interpret the words. Russ put the letter down and was just completely taken back. He could not say anything.

By now I came down the steps and had put on a different shirt, modeled it for Russ. I asked, "Is this alright? Can we go now?" The two of us left to go out to the car.

I could feel that Russ was not Russ, he hadn't made one comment, nor joke, and finally I asked, "Russ are you all right?"

It was obvious Russ was just reaching for words.

I asked again, "Russ, what the hell is the matter with you?"

Russ looked very misty eyed. That floored me. I mean this is Russ who, in the eye of danger, was able to make a joke…say something witty. Him sitting there, now just looking in space…I stopped in the driveway and turned around and looked at Russ again. "Russ, are you all right?"

Russ just couldn't contain himself anymore. He said, "George, I never thought you had any feelings at all – none. The way you deal with things and the way you deal with people, I always thought you were a perfect machine. I never realized that anyone meant that much to you, nevertheless a woman."

I didn't quite understand what Russ was talking about. I asked again, "Russ, what the hell is the matter with you?"

He replied, "That stupid schoolteacher. Man, I didn't know you..." and he didn't finish the sentence. We both got into the car as the driver shut the door and got in behind the steering wheel.

I sat there and looked at Russ.

While we were staring at each other, the driver was waiting to be told where they were going for dinner. Finally, I gave him the name of the restaurant...Rio Limo...that was the restaurant where the whole experience started. I kept looking at Russ. "Russ, please what the hell is wrong with you? I don't like seeing you like this."

Russ's response was blurted out. "You know, I read your letter!"

I didn't know whether to be mad or what emotion I was supposed to show. I felt much betrayed and yet relieved...I didn't know what I felt but it was as though Russ had crawled inside my brain.

Russ just sat, but finally continued. "Man, I don't know what the hell to say."

I sat back and almost whispered. "Let's just forget it. I mean, one of us has got to. Me I'm going to try. Although I'll never succeed, I'm still going to try...certainly you should be able to, so forget about it. It's one of those things that you go through. You don't really know what life would have been if things had worked out differently. I don't know if the person I'm thinking about would be the same person who actually is..."

Russ said, "You know, everything you're saying is very true. And I guess if I had put more weight into the things you were telling me; I would be able to now say, 'Well, that's the way life is. It sucks." But that's not what happened. You were going through a hell and I was making fun of it, if not to you, to myself."

I cut him off. "Russ, wait a minute, this is completely out of character for you. Now, please, don't get into some God damn philosophical discussion."

Russ said, "No, no, no, I'm not being philosophical, I'm just telling you I feel like a goddamn heel. Here I am joking around and this thing is really eating at you."

I said, "You could tell all this from a goddamn letter, that isn't even a letter?"

He replied, "George, I didn't even understand half of it. But, I know that what is there is sincere. But, where the hell did you ever come up with a goddamn phrase, 'It's got to be true, because there ain't a happy ending.' Man that's…that's like out there."

"You know, Russ, I'm very sorry you read the goddamn letter now, believe me…"

Russ interrupted. "Well, I'm not."

We just stared and looked at each other and spent the rest of the trip to the restaurant in silence. The driver finally got to the restaurant. We got out and started to walk in the door, when I grabbed Russ' arm and said, "Russ, going to dinner with you now is different, man. I like the old Russ much better."

Russ said, "You know what? After reading what you've been through, I don't like the old Russ at all. And, I don't know. Well, I think I'm going to."

Each sentence Russ said wasn't completed. He just stopped talking and left it hanging in mid air.

I shook my head and said, "Boy." But, I didn't know what the hell to do. When we got inside the restaurant we waited to be seated, the hostess came over, who was about 6'6", very slender built, very muscular though. It was very obvious she worked out. She walked up and wanted to seat us. Russ looked up and had to lean back to see her, went over, got a chair, pulled it by her, stood on the chair. The hostess was standing there; she didn't know what the hell he was doing.

He opened his arms and hugged her and said, "I want you to know, I love you. I'm not going to hide it, I'm going to tell you straight out, I love you. I don't care what I have to do, what mountain I got to climb…" By now, two waiters started to come over. I was just standing and laughing.

I grabbed Russ and said, "Get the hell off that chair."

The hostess was just bright red. The two waiters arrived and I turned to them and said, "Gentlemen, unless you are very brave men, I suggest you go back to what you were doing. Believe me; you got the wrong person, go back to where you were."

The hostess regained her composure and led Russ and me to a table. The two waiters followed us to the table, not saying a word.

After we were seated I said, "Russ, what the hell did you do that for?"

He said, "George, this evening was starting off on a bad note and I figure if I did something it would snap you back to you, whatever the hell that is, and me back to me. And it looked like it worked so don't yell."

The waiter arrived and we ordered dinner. That was the end. That was the end of the discussion for the evening.

A week went by before I got a phone call from Russ. "George, pal!" he yelled into the phone. "You know I was thinking about you and, well, listen, why we don't get together for lunch tomorrow?"

I thought for a minute and said, "You're on, and I'm not doing anything."

Russ replied in his usual jovial tone, "Good, don't get the driver, just you and I will go. I'll drive. I'll drive. I'll come over and get you and I'll drive."

I was first taken back since usually Russ wasn't that accommodating, but I said "okay" and we agreed to meet the following day about noon. At the appropriate time, Russ was at the house banging on the door. Russ had an aversion for using doorbells. Remembering our last outing I was wearing a sport shirt and a jacket. Russ came in, but he had a very drawn look about him.

I said, "Russ, you know you got one big problem, pal. When something's bugging you, you wear it on sleeve."

Russ said, "Yeah, yeah, I know, but…well come on let's go. I'll tell you over lunch."

So, I said, "Well, why don't we just sit down here? I can call up a local restaurant. They'll deliver here. And tell me what the hell is bothering you."

Russ thought about it a minute. "Would you mind? Would you mind? I'll call, wait, I'll call. Wait, you got their number?"

I went over to my desk and took out the number of the local restaurant. Russ quickly called and put an order in and we sat down and I waited quietly for Russ to start talking. Finally, Russ was sitting on one chair and…on another…Finally, I half yelled, "Russ, stop moving, you're making me dizzy…Look at you! Now what the hell is the matter with you? And stop all this moving around!"

"I went and found her," he replied. "There's a problem though."

"Okay, what the hell is the problem?" I asked in an annoyed tone.

"She is a very bad sick. They had to do one of them operations, you know, when they stick a balloon in you, what the hell ever it is." Russ hesitated. "Well, that's where she's at. She's at the hospital and it doesn't look too good."

I was in shock, but managed to say, "Russ, what the hell did you do, go see her?"

Russ, nodding his head, replied, "Well yeah, but she don't know I was there. She was whacked out. I took her medical chart…I made a copy of it and I went to our friend, you know the doctor and I asked him to explain it to me. He said it seem like everything went okay, it's just that she just…they want to try to get her the hell up, but she ain't moving. And they're afraid she'll get pneumonia or something, I don't know. But she'll get something but she won't get it if she gets the hell up. She just has no will to get up."

I said, "Russ, wait, my god! You're telling me you robbed the goddamn medical chart?"

Russ fired back, "Well, I made a copy of them, what the hell is the big deal? They got theirs, I got mine."

I could not believe what I was hearing. "That's crap. Well, forget about it, I mean Jesus Christ. You know what hospital she's at?"

"Yeah, yeah, yeah," Russ responded.

While we were still bantering back and forth, the ringing of the doorbell was a welcome relief in the discussion we were having, as the restaurant had delivered the lunch order. Russ, true to his word, paid the delivery boy, closed the door and promptly walked into the kitchen to set up our lunch.

I was following him. "Would you stop with the goddamn…with that lunch?"

Russ, still setting the table responded, "Well, sit down, sit down, have something to eat. And…we'll decide what you want to do."

I was really annoyed as I inquired, "Well, what the hell am I going to do? I'm going to walk in, say 'Hi, surprise. After a hundred years, I'm here!"

Russ, nodding his head and still chewing, responded, "Well, I got a feeling if you don't do that, you're going to feel worse than you feel right now. I did the best I could."

I looked at him with a half smile, "You know Russ, you're right. You did. All right, well I'm going to go…I don't know what the hell to do right now!"

Russ continued to eat and talk. "You know, she got a couple

of kids! They're in their forties. Yeah, yeah they are. Well, they're not forty, but they're close to it. They came in because things are pretty grave. So, I don't know when the hell they go but if you want, I'll go down first. I'll find if anybody's in. Afterwards, if everything is clear, you'll go in...You don't do anything else. You walk in and say 'good-bye.' You can look up in the sky and say, 'Someday we'll meet up in the great beyond.'"

Still in shock, I responded, "You know something, Russ...you know when you do things like this, I don't know...you drive me out of my goddamn mind."

"George," he said. "Hey look, I went... here's the information that's where she's at. If you want to go, go. If you don't want to go, don't go. But Jesus Christ you can't go on writing letters. I mean, that's nuts. And besides, they don't work. You're just driving yourself nuts and me too."

Russ could see I wasn't listening...he thought that he was not wanted, took his hold of the sandwich that he had ordered for lunch and said, "I'm not staying here with you. You're a drag. I'll talk to you!" Russ left.

I was sitting down at the table, trying to figure out what I was going to do and finally, as though a light went on inside me, I just said, "Who the hell am I kidding!" I threw the rest of the sandwich away and went upstairs to change into a blue suit, white shirt and tie. I started driving down to the hospital. I didn't quite know where it was, but I knew it was down in South Jersey area.

I called for information and worked my way with the telephone and finally found out where the hospital was and directions on how to get there. Surprisingly by the time I called, I was very close. It was within five minutes after I called that I was at the hospital. I parked the car, got out and started to walk towards the front door. I was still rather reluctant to go, only because I felt my mere presence might create a problem that I didn't want to create. No matter what, every time I took one step forward, I decided not to go. I absolutely resolved that I wasn't going. I felt it was really stupid for me to do this. The next thing I knew, I was in the elevator going up to the floor she was on. Russ, of course, had provided all the necessary information as to how to get in without anybody seeing me, and what room to go to plus all the other specific details. Russ had written down everything on the piece of paper that he stuck in my pocket just before he left. Everything was true to form, even the directions on how to get there. I felt foolish for having called information. I walked into the room, not really knowing what to expect, but after going to the hospital to see many other people, one gets to accept anything in a hospital. I looked down and there was this frail lady lying in the bed. She just turned over to look up and she knew who I was. She didn't know my name at first, but a smile started to come across her face as I looked down at her. Neither one of us said a word. We both knew who the other person was. I didn't know what to say, but somebody had to say something because the silence that was in the room was a weight on both of us.

I started and with half a smile on my face said, "You know, I guess I had envisioned meeting you in bed, but this wasn't exactly what I had in mind." My comment brought an appropriate half smile.

She responded, "Oh George."

I was stunned that she knew my name.

She said, "It's been a long time."

I managed to speak even though my throat was dry. I said, "Yeah, yeah well, I'm not going to be stupid enough to ask how you're doing, because you don't look too good in that bed, kid. Come one, why don't you get up 'cause I can't stand this room? We'll go to the solarium out here, down the hall, okay?" She nodded. I was remembering the phrase in the chart that I had read saying that it would be best for her to get up. But, she wanted to stay in bed.

"No," she said. "I can't. I'm tired."

I was trying to be stern, but the tears in my eyes had a quieting effect. "What the hell are you talking about, you're tired? Get up out of that bed. Come on. Don't deny me this…this one time that I'm around when you need a little help and not let me give it. Please, don't do that to me!"

She thought about it a second. "Well," she said, "I just don't have the strength."

I said, "That's okay. I got the strength for the both of us. Come on." She was fumbling around looking for something and pointing to her bathrobe. I promptly got it and handed it to her.

She said, "Well, go outside. I'll…I'll…"

"All right," I said as I pulled the curtain around the bed for her to get dressed. Within a few minutes I heard the rustling sounds of someone getting dressed and I heard my name being called. I went back in and there she was sitting up in bed with her bathrobe on. I was stunned. I pushed the curtain back and put out my arm for her to hold on to. I said, with a smile on my face, "Where the hell did you get this bathrobe? It's nice, but…don't worry about it, I'll get you a new one."

In a very stern voice, she replied, "You will not." Her response startled me, because of the volume it was said with.

"What do you mean, I won't? I'll get you one of them really classy ones with fur on it, you know."

"I happen to like this. I'll wear this," she responded. The words were not said in a frail tone, but rather with some strength behind them. She got up, hanging on my arm, and we started walking out of the room and into the hallway to go down to the solarium.

The nurses at the nurse station saw them coming out and were dumbfounded. One turned to the others and asked, "Who the hell is that?"

The other nurse said, "I don't know, but my God, whoever

he is, he got her up from that bed!"

The two of us made our way towards the solarium. Slow, but still at a steady pace.

Betsy looked up and said, "George, this is just…"

I interrupted. "I wouldn't hear of this…Look, why are you trying to rain on my parade?"

She replied, "What do you mean your parade?"

"What's the problem?" I asked "Here we are taking a walk, it's a nice day, walking arm in arm. Now don't start shattering it with a lot of complaints 'cause I don't want to hear any. You know, whatever the doctors did, they did, and you're okay. You're in tip-top shape. The doctor's claim after one of those operations, your blood will flow better. You should be jumping around. Instead you're still in the goddamn bed."

Betsy stopped. "Now, how did you know I was here?"

I flushed, and half laughing said, "Well, don't worry about that."

"No, I want to know!" she fired back. Now the words were said in a stronger voice.

I could just feel her getting stronger. "Well, I'm not going to tell you. Who the hell are you to question me?"

She let go of me, turned, and faced me… She felt uneasy and I grabbed her and said, "Now easy girl, easy. If you're going to try, you got to wait till you get a little stronger on your pins. Come on, are you all right? You feel all right?"

She nodded. "Oh, just please, I could just… I could just die."

Her words stung me. "What the hell are you talking about? Dying? What do you mean anyway? Isn't everybody's dream to die in the arms of someone who loves them?"

She stood straight up now, by herself, and looked at me. "I would never put it quite that way."

I said, "Well, come on….We'll go to the atrium. We'll sit in there. We'll sit down, and you'll see, it will be nice."

We kept working our way towards the lounge chairs by a window in the solarium. When reaching them, I lowered her into the seat. She went searching through he pockets for her comb. She found it and started to fix her hair, straightened her glasses and straightened her outfit. I stood there and smiled.

She looked up and said, "You must think this is very funny. I must look horrible."

I replied, "Yes. I mean, don't get me wrong, I love the way you look, and you're beautiful to me. You fix yourself the way you want and you go and do this act, I love it."

She said, "What do you mean act? Do you think I'm acting just to get people's sympathy?"

Again, the words seem to build upon the prior word. Two nurses from the nurses' station had positioned themselves right outside the solarium so they could look in and hear what was going on, but yet, could not be seen.

"That's a little rude of you. I mean, what is the matter with you? Do you think I would be acting like this if I felt good?" The tone of her voice was much stronger now.

I hesitated before I replied. "You just got to move around a little more...there you are...determined to stay in that stupid bed. I mean, not that I'm against lying in bed, but I don't think it should be done under these circumstances."

We sat there for a while before she started again. "You know, you absolutely amaze me. You really, truly, think I would act like this if I was feeling better?"

I said, "Well, you know, let's face facts. I thought about you a lot, but this is the first time I ever met you in a long time and, you know, so far, what can I tell you? Don't get dizzy now. You know, make believe you're going to faint or anything like that."

She said, "No, I'm not going to do any of those things."

"Well, good," I replied. "Now, do you want to hear my life story?"

For the next few minutes we spent in the exchange of the

normal cardinalities between two old strangers.

"George," she said. "There was never a 'we.' I never felt the same way about you, the way you feel about me. There never was a 'we' and there will never be a 'we.' I wish you would now leave and never think about me again. Please, don't write to me, call me or try to contact me in anyway."

All the light, sound and air left the room. I sat there with Betsy in a vacuum that the words she said had just created. The next thing I knew, I saw her changing color right before my eyes. I stood there and I didn't know what to do. I sat down on the chair next to her. I got up and walked out the door. I never looked back. Two nurses saw me leaving and went in to the room.

I go to the door to go, but I couldn't go and I just knew I couldn't stay. I was in this suspended animation in my own mind. I left the building in a hypnotic state. I knew I had to go home. When I walked in my door at home the phone was ringing. It was Russ. I suddenly realized that I had left the hospital and drove home in a trance.

"Well, what happened?" he asked.

Before I fully realized what I was saying, I told him the whole story. When I was done, I looked at the phone.

Russ was silent, but finally he said, "Man I didn't know it would end like this." He hung up the phone before I could respond. I stood there until the dial tone brought me back to reality. I hung up the phone. I, too, thought to myself, I never thought it would end like this.

I walked over to my desk, picked up the letter, folded it neatly in four parts and promptly tore it up. I said out loud, "Whatever I feel must end. I don't think it ever will until I die. Certainly I have to at least make a step towards putting her out of my mind, 'cause, writing didn't mean a damn thing. It still hurts and I guess it will be an injury, a hurt I will feel the rest of my life." I shut the lights and went to bed hoping that sleep would come. Instead, I kept thinking about all the things I should have done and things I should have said. I finally realized that love can come in a second and can't be forgotten in a lifetime. That Cardinal was right. I will never heal, but he also assured me that there would be an answer that would somehow help me live with the hurt. A verse started going through my thoughts, first slowly and at an ever-increasing speed.

As I lay in my bed and thought what would be
I felt as though I was in a great sea
For I didn't know what was in store for me
I quickly realized the future was not for me to see
As I think back now to times long ago
Certain truths appear as though in a glow
It's a part, we were, but why I don't know
And tomorrow will pass for that too will go
As the nighttime comes and out the window I see
The blackness appears as the daylight does flee
And the air begins to stir all around me
The rhythmic beat of the cars and that makes three
As I feel the loneliness monster within me creep
I no longer fear it nor does it make we weep
The monster is gone; I do not have to sleep
As the great joy within me does leap
I no longer wonder what there will be
I enjoy it now for I hold the key
For in my mind's eye I can now see
At long last there will be a "We"
I can create the dream and put you with me
But now I have won the victory I see
For, I didn't know what was in store for me
I quickly realized the future was not for me to see
I no longer wonder what there will be
I enjoy it now for I hold the key

For in my mind's eye I can now see
At long last there will be a "We"
With sound, black and air for the three
I can create the dream and put you with me
It was fear and loneliness at first there would be
But now I have won the victory I see
For at last I have won my internal strife
It is sad but it's true you're not with me in life
Your absences from me was like a knife
It is sad, but it's true you were never my wife
In my mind where you first appear
In my heart your presence I did fear
I now know the secret of bring you near
For now you're inside me that is clear
I have only to look inward and alone we will be
So I close my eyes for the blackness the first of the three
My heart makes the rhythmic beat, as I need it, you see
The last is the air that's the third and I'm free
For it is the only place where Betsy's with me.

As I laid my head back down on the pillow and became determined to forget her, I thought to myself, "Of course, there is always the ever-present possibility that I don't want to forget her and that is the scariest part of all."

How much simpler it would be if we could just put our lives on tape and play it on a VCR machine. We could stop it...rewind it...redo the parts we didn't like...or if all else failed, erase it and start all over again. No matter how I try, the bleak face of reality puts me back to the point where I don't know what to do, or better yet, even if I do what I want, all the people around me would have to reprogram their lives to accommodate my changes.

By far, the hardest part is facing reality and feeling your strength being sapped by age and human frailties. To be reminded of each passing day, that the next time you're going to see someone is as you're looking down at them in their coffin or looking up at them from yours, somehow wears like a heavy yoke.

This may be the final sentence of the final chapter, but as long as I have any conscious thought process, I don't think it will be the end to what I feel or at least I hope it isn't.

The journey ends. The hurt stops. The only thing to look forward to is meeting God and finding out why he punished me so. Sleep finally came.

# Chapter Nineteen

The next morning I felt reborn. I was mad at myself for feeling helpless. I reasoned that we could never have children, so what did I really want from her? I answered the question almost as quickly as I asked it. I want her to come to Italy with me back to the spot where I first saw her coming out of the water.

Why should she come?

I sat at my desk wondering if there was any way I would be able to convince Betsy to come to Italy with me. A wish of her coming with me, which had turned to a desire, had now become an obsession. It was very obvious that she wanted no part of me no matter what scenario I devised. I could only guess that her reason was precipitated by her experiences in life. I really didn't know if that was true or that she found me too repulsive to be with. Either way I knew there was no way she was coming to Italy with me.

I thought that without going into great detail I would ask other people's opinions as to what they thought I should do. I discarded that idea, for I just knew that everyone I asked would see through my trying to make the question sound as though I was asking for a friend. I could use the reason that I could not go into any greater detail. I just dropped the topic with the lame reason that I really didn't know too much more than I had already said. That would be too obvious. Anyway I would probably ask the wrong people. The people I knew were too smart and I didn't trust them to not betray my confidence.

My examination and re-examination of the problem just kept me going in circles. A problem without an answer was neither something I was used to nor one that I would accept. I listed the reasons why someone would want to go with me, but as I stared at the blank piece of paper it became painfully obvious that I couldn't come up with a reason.

Suddenly, the answer came to me. A contract! I would write a contract for her to be my escort in Italy. I would send her a letter spelling out the terms and conditions. Separate rooms plus a per diem allowance for incidentals. Meals included. Time off each day to be alone if that is what she wanted. The tour would include any place she wanted to go with my only choice being the resort outside of Salerno where I had seen her. I thought of adding a visit to the Cardinal but decided against it. I had a strong feeling of jealousy for having to share her with anyone. I was embarrassed at my own stupidity. I was convinced that a contract would be the answer.

As I sat back feeling proud of my accomplishment, a strange thought came to mind. What if she said "no," or worse yet, she said nothing? She never responded to anything I sent her, why should she respond to a contract? I felt more desperate than before. I resolved that if I didn't get an answer within a few weeks I would send her another letter, but in the second one I would put: "If you don't come with me, I will find your daughter and convince her that I am her father and I stood away from her all of these years because of my love for her mother and my desire to make her mother 'happy.' Perfect.

I sat back in my chair and realized that what I was thinking was a horrible thing to do but I just didn't see any other alternative. I spoke to the wall in front of me as I said, "The way I see it, I can only break even. You hate me now and I can't believe you hating me even more is going to change anything."

I would end the letter with, "Call me with your decision."

I quickly wrote the letter in long hand as I felt that would make it more personal. I folded it neatly and placed it in a stamped envelope and started walking to the mail box on the corner. Half-way there I stopped for the thought came to me, "What if her daughter wanted proof?"

I stood in the middle of the sidewalk as I pondered the problem. I'll dig up her father and get a DNA sample from him. Problem solved. I continued towards the mail box.

Maybe I should call Russ and ask his opinion?

I stood for a moment with the letter half in the slot but resolved there was no other way. As I turned to walk back home I heard the metal lid on the mail box close. My letter was on the way. The sound was deafening. I walked home knowing that my faith was sealed.

# About the Author

George Delmarmo is a retired accountant and attorney living in Brick, New Jersey. He has traveled extensively while representing an international list of clientele. His experiences varied to all types of assignments that required his special mixture of talents. He started writing to fill the void in his life created by his retirement. He has written a series of books, which are a reflection of his travels and experiences. He is a member of the New Jersey as well as the New York bars and is a licensed accountant in the State of New Jersey.

Memoirs of a Retired Modern Day Mercenary, George.

George is a retired mercenary who at the end of his career started writing his memoirs.

To contact George please send an email to:

**hogfarmer@.aol.com**

# Books by George Delmarmo

*A Heart Never Heals*: The story of a girl George sees in a vision. She appeared to George while in Italy working on a case. She was walking out of the Mediterranean Sea. The vision is so vivid that he visits the Vatican to confer with a Cardinal seeking an explanation of what he saw. The Cardinal advises George to start from the very beginning of the events of what brought him to that spot at that time. George relates the details of his journey. When George returns home he finishes the case before he starts on his maddening quest to find his vision.

*All About Mary*: The story about the extent that the police will go to entrap someone. The tactics police use when used against them creates the backdrop of the story. Emotions such as love and affection are used like any other tool. The legality of an act is only a wisp of air and so many words when the party in charge tries to use them for their own benefit. The main character is an attorney in the prosecutor's office who changes her name and her persona in order to get her man. The results she achieves winds up being her own downfall.

*Cooperstown Diamonds*: The story of a man who lived his life to the fullest by manipulating everyone one around him. He was the kind of man who lived his life according to his rules and somehow everyone just let him do what he wanted. By using his personal charm and cunning built for himself his own World and loved every minute of it. He would be accused of many things but with the help of his friend was never found guilty of any wrong doing. He could play his life as one would play a fiddle, just for his pleasure.

***The Darkest Day***: Deals with a family's problems of Divorce and Abortion. It also deals with a woman who decides that she is going to become the matriarch of the family. Her domination destroys the family for no one in the family wants her to assume such a role. What the members of her family want are secondary to her unmerciful quest to become the dominant factor. She learns too late the folly of her choices. The financial viability and the stability of her family are destroyed before her very eyes but this does not deter her from her quest.

***Deception by Marriage***: The story of a man and woman who use marriages as a method of getting what they want out of life. They have no regard for the human tragedy they leave behind. They have no sympathy or concern for the people around them. Divorce and abandonment are used as tools and a convenient method of getting in and out of situations that no longer interest them. The children as well as spouses they leave behind are of no concern to them as they go through life searching for what they feel will satisfy them for the moment.

***End of the Light***: The story deals with one man's encounter with the supernatural. The love of one man is traced throughout his life and the life of the woman he loved. Their affection for each other lasted throughout both their lives. Although she died years before him he was still close to her until his death that occurred years later. After her death her spirit stayed in the lighthouse where they first met until he joined her. Try as he may he could not forget or get away from her. The story is sad for he never wanted to.

***Hate Crimes***: The story revolves around a group of people who use the acts of the police to create a resort type setting. People are invited to participate in some of the infamous shootouts. The story examines the actions of police and criminals alike. After studying them, the acts are used to train a group of people to enforce what should be done rather than what the law allows. The training of different groups of people blends in with the resort type atmosphere that the story is set in. The training is sometimes used to thwart the police's efforts to stop crimes.

***It Begins... It Ends***: The story of a murder case set in an actual setting. It shows the investigating and defending of a suspect while life still goes on. Although a lawyer takes on a case his on personal life as well of his associates still continues. Each element of the story is set in the middle of all the activities that take place as an ordinary part of living. The story also points out the errors that can be made in gathering evidence. These errors whether done by omission or commission can get a person convicted. The story stresses the defense attorney's job.

***Last of the Last***: The story of a man who pleaded guilty to a crime he didn't commit. At the time he did it was cheaper to do so than to go through a trial. After the plea is entered the government changes the terms of the plea. The change deals with the prison he will be sent to. The man decided to agree to the terms anyway. He contracts a fatal disease. The closer he gets to death's door the more he can't deal with his plea as a mark on his soul. George is hired to have the guilty plea set aside.

***Mississippi After Dark***: The story of a series of unexplained disappearances and deaths. The police feared that a serial killer might be responsible. He had to be stopped. The question was how. No outsider law enforcers were welcomed in the state least of all the FBI. The state was concerned with their public image if the story leaked out to the media. They did not want the federal government serial killer division officially involved. The State's concern was created by the popularity of the movie, Mississippi Burning. George was hired to quietly find the killer and to end the killings.

***Outraged in Mexico***: The story of a town and its people caught up in violence and manipulation of a system that was ruled by one man. When they could take no more they rebelled against the tyranny and recaptured their lives. The retribution they took against those who enslaved them and the effort the people put forth to rebuild their lives is what makes up the basis for the story. The people involved are constantly forced to decide what values they want to nurture and what to disregard. They are forced to change their values to rid themselves of their oppressors.

***Rape***: The story of a young man who is accused of Rape. The case causes the boy and girl to examine their own minds as to whether or not a rape occurred in the legal sense and in the moral sense. The state becomes so relentless in their quest to convict the boy that they forget that their job is also to protect the innocent. The ethnic and religious backgrounds of the two people is difficult to keep out of the case as they are both caught up in the whirlwind  that is created whenever the crime of Rape is charged.

***2.8 Seconds***: The story of an alleged plot to assassinate the Pope during his visit to Venezuela. The people of the country were divided as to the value of having the Holy Father visit the country. George was hired to find the people involved as well as make sure that the assassination did not take place. Neither the church officials nor the authorities wanted to be connected to the investigation in anyway. His assignment also was to include developing an assassination plan that circumvented all the precautions taken by both the church as well as the government security forces.

***When God Ain't Lookin'***: The story covers the life time of two people meeting, parting and reuniting again. The characters are from two different worlds. Ann is a nun who is not sure she wants to be a nun because of the hypocrisy she found in her order. Although twenty-five when she first meets George she looks much younger. George is a twenty year old young man when they meet and has no idea that he is dating an older woman who is a nun. Their meetings over the years cause much joy and sadness for both of them.

***Yellow River:*** The story of the "Enforcers" leaving Hong Kong when it was returned to Chinese rule. They were the Chinese who helped the English control Hong Kong during England's rule. The "Enforcers" were hated by their own countrymen and feared by everyone else in the world. They feared nothing. They had no ties to any Faith, Family or Country. They were ruthless and yet well educated by watching the British. The "Enforcers" were allowed to leave Hong Kong and enter Canada and America as long as they were penniless. They had to find different ways to bring their wealth with them.